Two Gentlemen on the Beach

Two Gentlemen on the Beach

MICHAEL KÖHLMEIER

Translated by Ruth Martin

Originally published as *Zwei Herren Am Strand* by Michael Köhlmeier
© 2014 Carl Hanser Verlag, München

First published in English in 2016 by
HAUS PUBLISHING LTD.
70 Cadogan Place, London SW1X 9AH
www.hauspublishing.com

English Translation Copyright © Ruth Martin 2016

ISBN: 978-1-910376-46-1
eISBN: 978-1-910376-47-8

Typeset in Garamond by MacGuru Ltd

Printed and bound in Spain by Liberduplex

A CIP catalogue for this book is available from the British Library

For Michael Krüger

Little man: "I've got an umbrella."

"That's a nice umbrella. Nice and big."

Little man: "But it's not raining."

"True. You have an umbrella because it might rain. Seems like it's going to, as well. Look at those black clouds!"

Little man: "If it rains, I'm not going to put my umbrella up."

"Why not? I mean, you'll get wet, and your umbrella can save you from getting wet, and when you're wet, when you're soaked through, you can easily get sick."

Little man: "I'm not putting my umbrella up because it's new."

"Are you afraid it might get broken?"

Little man: "If I don't put it up, it won't break."

"You're right there. But then you might as well leave it at home."

Little man: "If I leave it at home, people will ask me if I don't have an umbrella."

Monika Helfer, *Die Bar im Freien* (The Outdoor Bar)

PART ONE

1

On Christmas Day 1931, at around midday – so my father told me – a man was standing on the front steps of the house at 119 East 70th Street in Manhattan, New York. He had come to visit Mr Winston Churchill, who was residing there temporarily with his cousin.

The visitor didn't have an appointment. Neither the butler nor the nurse knew him, and in their eyes the fact that he claimed to be Charlie Chaplin marked him out as a dangerous lunatic. They threatened to call the police, and the butler finally fetched a Brown Bess musket – which, admittedly, was not in working order; it was one of a pair of mementos from the War of Independence that usually hung above the coat rack in the lobby. It was only when the man cupped his hands around his mouth and shouted as loudly as he could – which was not very loudly – through the crack in the door where he had jammed his knee: "Winston! Winston! It's me, Charlie. I'm here, Winston! I came!" – and Churchill, who fortunately had a room on the ground floor, shouted back, as loudly as he could – which at that time was not very loudly, either – "Glad tidings you bring!" that he was permitted to enter.

Churchill was sitting up in bed. In front of him was a pastry board that he was using as a writing tray, and on it were his hand-written notes, a fountain pen and some coloured pencils. In the corner stood an easel taller than a man, and a table covered in tubes, brushes, bottles and pots. There was a pile of books beside his pillow. His torso was bare, his left shoulder and the left half of his chest bandaged, and his arm and throat were yellow with old bruises.

Chaplin recalled: "Tears spilled from his eyes."

Ten days previously, Churchill had been in an accident. Unusually for him, he had been alone, on foot, on 76th Street. On this surprisingly mild winter afternoon, he had been intending to cross Fifth Avenue and take a stroll through Central Park, where he was to meet Bernard Baruch, his friend and financial advisor, in the Museum of Natural History. The two of them – it was a long-standing arrangement that had been put off several times – were planning to take a look at the *Star of India*, the world's largest sapphire, before dining together at Baruch's apartment. Lost in thought, Churchill looked to the right, as he would have done in England, stepped out into the road, and was hit by a car and thrown onto the sidewalk. His shoulder, face, hip and left thigh were badly injured. The driver of the car that hit him, an Italian-born electrician, was the first on the scene, and it was he who went for an ambulance. Churchill was taken to nearby Lennox Hill Hospital, where they kept him for a week despite his protestations. The doctors also diagnosed a concussion: his balance was affected, rapid eye movement meant he was temporarily unable to see, and he was sick several times.

A nurse's indiscretion led to the press getting wind of the matter. The doctors unanimously refused to speak to the reporters, who avenged themselves by inventing things. One day the *New York Times* said that Churchill was doing well under the circumstances, sending best wishes from his sickbed to the kind electrician from Napoli who had taken such good care of him; the following day's *Wall Street Journal* reported that Churchill was hovering between life and death. The *New York Journal* even suggested he would probably never walk again, and almost certainly never speak again – at any rate, it said, his political career was over. The reports were picked up by newspapers and radio stations all over the world. In London, the Dean of Westminster called on the cathedral's congregation to pray for him.

At that point, Chaplin was in Britain. Following the English premiere of *City Lights* at the Dominion Theatre in London at the end
of February, he and his entourage had travelled across Europe, visiting Berlin, Munich, Venice, Vienna, Paris, and taking a limousine
along the Atlantic coast to Aquitaine. He met his brother Sydney
in the South of France and persuaded him to join the party. They
crossed to Algiers on the newly-launched Italian luxury steamer
Augustus, where they were received by another half a dozen friends,
and finally drove through North Africa in a convoy of four rough-
and-ready jeeps.

Churchill and Chaplin had already met twice that year: in
London after the film premiere – it was a meeting Chaplin didn't
care to recall – and more or less by chance in September, in Biarritz. And they had found the time to be alone together and conduct
long conversations, about which they maintained absolute silence.
This made the English journalists, renowned for their curiosity,
livid and inclined to speculation. The sympathetic ones claimed the
two of them were planning a film project, while others hinted that
the artist and the politician were mixed up in some shady stock-
market deal, and the malicious ones scented some kind of Jewish
conspiracy. For a time, the society pages of the British newspapers
were full of gossip about this odd couple, though no "reliable"
information was to be found there. The protagonists had sworn a
scout's-honour oath not to tell anyone about their walks and talks
together.

Churchill also travelled a lot that year, staying in France and
Germany. He had spent the autumn at home at Chartwell, his
country house, which looked out over the Weald of Kent. There
he had found himself "in the best possible mood," as he wrote
to the architect Philip Tilden, even though his political career
seemed to have reached its end: he had once again fallen out with
the Conservative leadership, and had not been considered for any
political office following the October election. "I intend to make

a lot of money as an author," he wrote – and you can almost hear the commanding tone in his voice. "This is where my talent and my vocation lie. I will go down in history as a writer, not a politician." It is true that at this point – he was fifty-eight – the greater part of his income came from the columns and articles he wrote for newspapers and magazines all over the world, and the royalties from his books (which included *The World Crisis*, his four-volume history of the 1914–1918 war, and *My Early Life*, the memoirs of his youth, both of them bestsellers). Now he had a new project: the biography of his ancestor John Churchill, the first Duke of Marlborough, who had succeeded in uniting the powers of Europe against the political hegemony of the French King Louis XIV at the start of the eighteenth century. Rehabilitating the duke, who had fallen out of favour with historians, had been a dream of his as a young man. When Churchill set off for America in December, he had already dictated and corrected two hundred pages.

Chaplin meant to stay in London over Christmas, and return to the warmth of California in the New Year. The papers said the film star was planning a Christmas party for the orphans of the Hanwell Schools, where he himself had spent the loneliest and most bitter part of his childhood. He had paid the schools a visit, and had been overwhelmed by the love with which the boys and girls received him – "and not as a Hollywood star, but as one of their own", he told a reporter. (In all likelihood, this was reported accurately.) When he heard about Churchill's accident, he cancelled his attendance at the Christmas party at short notice, and booked a crossing to New York.

Chaplin mistrusted the horror stories. He knew from experience how much a certain kind of journalist enjoyed spreading lies in order to inflict pain on a once-celebrated personality. He was not overly worried for Churchill's life, nor even for his physical health. But he was fearful about his state of mind.

All of this I heard from my father.

2

My father had encountered Chaplin and Churchill as a child, both of them in our small town, and both at the same time; they had paid attention to him, spent time with him and praised him. Later on I would like very much to talk about this in greater detail. They were my father's idols in his youth and early adulthood; he could just as well imagine becoming a clown as a statesman. But what he became was a civil servant in the commune's food standards department, checking the milk from the surrounding farms, taking beer samples and measuring the sugar content of beet syrup.

After my mother's death, my father and I lived alone, a long way from any of our friends. When someone rang the doorbell we would remain sitting, silent and motionless, at the kitchen table. We got through the activities of the day as if we were parts of a machine for producing melancholy. (My first full-length performance – which wasn't until my late twenties – was actually entitled *The Melancholy Machine*: a man does his housework; everything goes wrong. I copied the face from Buster Keaton, the audience roared with laughter.) Then my father started drinking, and right from the start he drank a lot. One night I wrapped my arms around the unconscious man and dragged him into the bedroom, taking off his overcoat, jacket and shoes by the bed. At breakfast I said I didn't want to live any more. He cried, and stopped drinking.

After leaving school my father had wanted to study history, but the war had come between him and his plans. Now he intended to make up for what he had missed. During the worst period of his life, Churchill had saved himself by writing the biography of the First Duke of Marlborough; my father wanted to save himself

– and me – by writing the biography of Churchill. I was just starting school when he began. He told me about his work, and explained why he was doing it. When a person is very sad, he said, it is advisable for him to find some distraction from himself. There are a few very gifted people, he went on, who manage to pretend they're someone else: they look at themselves, shake their heads or nod their approval, and they take themselves seriously, but not too seriously; in this way they manage to get over their sadness without coming to any harm. But most people, he said, can only ever see themselves as just themselves – which is no wonder, because you *are* yourself, after all. These people can't pretend they're someone else. They have no choice but to pretend someone else is them. And that isn't so very difficult, my father said. It works best if you tell another person's life story. Churchill told the First Duke of Marlborough's life story; my father was going to tell Churchill's.

He learned English for this reason alone; he could read and write it, but he never spoke it well. When he came home from the office, he would read and study: he read late into the night; he read while I played beside him with my blocks; he read while I did my homework; he read while I cooked and piled stew onto our plates; he studied while he hung up the laundry, and while he did the ironing. He wasn't striving for any particular academic standard, but by the end of his life his historical knowledge would have put some university professors to shame.

Our town had more theatres and cinemas than other places did, and comedy was everywhere. My father thought he and his son were too lonely and laughed too little. He suggested going to the theatre or the cinema twice a week. I saw my first Chaplin film – *Limelight* – and my first clowns – Alfredo Smaldini, Arminio Rothstein (alias Habakuk), and the incomparable Charlie Rivel. I was interested in clowns, and my father said being a clown was a noble profession. He got me books full of biographies of famous comics, sketches, and instructions for pantomimes, and I tried to act out the numbers. We had some great evenings together. He would tell me what he had read, and what he was thinking of writing, and I would show him the comic turns I'd thought up. He laughed at my clowning like I had never seen him laugh before. We both laughed a lot during that time. I could imagine writing a biography of Charlie Chaplin when I grew up, just as he was – still, several years later – writing a biography of Winston Churchill.

I became a history and literature teacher at a selective school. At the weekends I performed as a clown, at first with a female colleague, and then alone. Later, when I gave up my teaching job and worked full-time as a clown, I had a life-sized puppet.

In autumn 1974, my father took part in a symposium in Aachen to mark Winston Churchill's 100th birthday. He was in the audience at the town hall when Mr William Knott – "The *very private* private secretary to a *very prime* prime minister" – was interviewed on stage by the journalist and Churchill biographer Sebastian Haffner. After the event, which took place in the hall where Churchill had received the Charlemagne Prize in 1956, my father approached this contemporary of Churchill's, a nondescript-looking man who seemed at once secretive and extroverted, caught him by the sleeve and addressed him in very formal English. Evidently the questions he asked were so original that Mr Knott was actually pleased to have been ambushed in this manner, and moreover accepted an invitation to lunch and a stroll the following day.

This encounter led to a correspondence that lasted a decade, until William Knott's death, with each of them writing two or three times a week, their letters frequently running to almost ten pages.

I gave these papers (more than 1000 pages) and a few photocopied documents to the Churchill Archives Centre in Cambridge, where they can be viewed from 9 to 5, Monday to Friday.

3

There was a reason that Chaplin and Churchill told nobody – not even their closest friends – about their "talk-walks", as the agile Chaplin called them, or "duck-walk-talks" in the corpulent Churchill's self-deprecating version of the phrase: namely, because they were talking about suicide.

They didn't linger on other matters. They had too few common interests and too many divergent views. They took short cuts, bypassing polite chit-chat, skirting around personal matters that didn't relate to their subject, and picking up again where their exchange of views had left off months, or sometimes years, previously. They discussed motives and techniques for taking one's own life, and contemplated the things that famous suicides had suffered and felt during the last days and hours of their lives: Vincent van Gogh, Seneca, Ludwig II of Bavaria, Lord Lyttleton, Hannibal and Jack London (whom Chaplin had known personally – London had given him the idea for *The Gold Rush*). They analysed their own states of mind in comparison with these examples. They were at all times aware that they needed consolation; they liked to complain to their nearest and dearest (both of them had a tendency towards pathos and weepiness) that they had been in need of consolation their whole lives. (To the astonishment of both men, they discovered that long before they had met, each of them had wanted to write a short essay on this notion. Though neither was aware of the other's intention, they had both been encouraged in this by T.S. Eliot. The famous poet, who was also plagued by depression, was planning an alphabet of consolation for the magazine *The Criterion*, in which Chaplin and Churchill's pieces would have appeared alongside each other. For some reason, nothing came of it.)

After just one meeting, they made a pact to see each other at least once a year, and walk together for at least two hours. Neither of them was a great walker, and they only paid attention to nature with its birds, flowers, scents and colours when it aligned with their aesthetic aims – Chaplin when he was in front of the camera, showing its effect in the Tramp's face, and Churchill when he was planning the garden at Chartwell, like a three-dimensional painting, accessible to all the senses, a thing of his own creation. During their walks, they forced themselves to pay attention to nature and regard it as something requiring neither their assistance nor their judgement, though – as they confessed to themselves, half amused, half dismayed – they couldn't articulate what they actually meant by nature. Once, as they were walking up a steep, narrow path through the Malibu Hills, they stopped beside a bush loaded with small, blood-red fruit. When, after several minutes, neither of them had said anything, Chaplin wondered aloud what the reason for their reverent silence was. Churchill replied, self-consciousness. Chaplin mused that they probably still had a long path ahead of them. At which Churchill turned and looked at the hills, with their covering of wispy grass, then turned back and nodded in the direction they were going, before commenting on the look and the nod: "This is our path! This one! Just to weaken your metaphor." One could only afford metaphors when they didn't concern the whole.

Consolation, they agreed, if it was to work and to endure, had to be planned – not unlike a proposal in the House of Commons or the building of a swimming pool; not unlike shooting a film. But the quality of a plan depended on how it was drawn up. They ordered – yes, ordered! – themselves to stick to a method that would entirely eliminate pathos, sentimentality, morality, anything weepy, anything smacking of bribery or fatalism, and all useless railing against God and the world. And they managed to talk about themselves and the possibility of doing away with themselves as if these were negotiations over a third person who was not present, whose thoughts and fate did not so much provoke their sympathy as awaken an academic or aesthetic interest in them. Churchill later remarked that, looking back, their conversations had been dominated by the passive mood: he and his friend did not *negotiate*, "there were negotiations"; they didn't *take* an academic interest, their interest "was awoken"; they didn't *feel* sympathy, it was "provoked". Chaplin summarised their attitude to these conversations with the phrase "sober all the way to enlightenment".

Their conversations were often funny, very funny. But the intention behind them was not. Sometimes they bore fruit: take the scene from *City Lights,* in which the rich man puts a rope around his neck, the end of which is attached to a heavy stone he intends to push into the water. The Tramp desperately tries to prevent him, and the whole thing ends with the Tramp falling in the water himself – this was a scene they had come up with together, when their friendship was just a few hours old.

So Chaplin knew that Churchill had periods of gloom and hopelessness – the "black dog", as Samuel Johnson termed this bastard child of errant impulses and contaminated brain chemistry. He knew that Churchill, the quintessential British swashbuckler, kept finding himself in the kennel of the beast without having been able to take any precautions against it. He knew that the animal attacked him from behind, and within a few hours would turn Churchill, the quintessential rhetorician, into a nervous stutterer who was soon rendered monosyllabic, with only one thing on his mind. Churchill had never spoken to anybody, not even his doctors, in more detail and with more honesty about this torment.

Churchill, in turn, knew about the anxiety that came over the world's greatest film artist in the days and weeks following the completion of a picture, enslaving him, crippling him, sometimes reducing him to speechlessness and leaving him feeling utterly destroyed. Neither of them had much time for philosophy, and certainly not German philosophy, but they did share Nietzsche's opinion that the idea of suicide was a powerful consolation, which could get you through many a bad night. (Neither of them could have cited the place where that was written.)

To prevent this most radical of consolations from ever becoming their *only* consolation, Churchill and Chaplin decided to keep meeting; if there was one person who could stop the other taking this path, then it was he, or he.

4

Their first meeting left Chaplin with a powerful feeling of gratitude; and because gratitude – like justice, freedom, courtesy and
a few other abstract nouns – was one of the fundamental things
associated with the Tramp, he valued it very highly.

The encounter took place in the mansion belonging to Marion
Davis, known as "The Beach House" or "Ocean House" in Santa
Monica. Miss Davies was the lover of the publisher and media
tycoon William Randolph Hearst, and had been for many years.
She had invited two hundred people to the grand unveiling of this
house with its one hundred rooms, all of them famous figures from
politics, film, business and academia. Chaplin hadn't wanted to go,
but Douglas Fairbanks and Mary Pickford, his most loyal friends in
Hollywood, had finally convinced him.

This was the spring of 1927 – a terrible time for Chaplin. His
second marriage was in pieces. Lita and her lawyers had instigated
the dirtiest divorce battle that the American press could remember (and they were providing plenty of ammunition for it). They
intended to ruin Chaplin, both financially and socially, and they
had good prospects of doing so. They weren't just suing him; they
were also suing his studio and his company, United Artists. They
issued restraining orders against the National Bank of Los Angeles,
the Bank of Italy, and other financial institutions where they suspected Chaplin had deposited parts of his fortune, which was one
of the largest in the film industry.

Rumours were spread that before and during his marriage,
Chaplin had often had sex with underage girls. There were screaming headlines about a certain Lillita Louise MacMurray, who had
fallen into the fiend's clutches at the age of fifteen. It soon emerged

that this person was none other than Chaplin's wife herself – the
one who was taking him to court. Her stage name was Lita Grey,
and in her day-to-day business she proudly and brazenly called
herself Lita Grey Chaplin. The newspapers didn't bother to
mention this embarrassing blunder, and of course they made no
apology – they were already onto the next scandal. During Lita's
first pregnancy, they said, Chaplin had dismissed her abruptly from
the cast of *The Gold Rush*, where she had been the female lead, and
replaced her with Georgia Hale, a sixteen-year-old beauty queen
from Chicago. He had also forced Lita to keep the birth of their
son a secret, to make sure this event didn't take away from a "much
more important one", namely the film's premiere. He had bribed a
doctor, the papers said, to record Charles Junior's date of birth as a
few days later. The youngest of Chaplin's lovers, they said, had been
not yet thirteen, a girl from a God-fearing family who had run away
from home after fighting with her father. Chaplin had picked the
weeping girl up off the kerb, taken her home with him and played
the kind uncle, which he doubtless had the talent to do. The girl,
now a woman, was quoted in the paper as saying he had lied to her,
telling her everything was ok: he'd been in touch with her father,
who Chaplin said had made a point of asking him to "take good
care of her". And so he did – though the newspaper refused to say
how, out of consideration for the sensibilities of its female readership. Chaplin complained, and the paper was ordered to print a
retraction. And so it did – in tiny lettering, on page 5, a year later.

In their crusade against him, Lita's lawyers and the reporters
had soon explored every possible level of tastelessness and chican-
ery. The indictment – which was leaked to the press – mentioned
Chaplin's mental cruelty towards his wife, and then described in
detail, with no consideration for the "sensibilities of the female
readership", certain sexual practices outlawed in the USA, which
he had apparently demanded from her on a nightly basis. The Fatty
Arbuckle scandal was fresh in the public's minds – he was a friend of

Chaplin's from the early days, whom the court had acquitted of the manslaughter of an actress during an orgy. Even so, his career was over, and he was a wreck. Lita and her lawyers were clearly trying to force Chaplin into the same corner: not only calling him a child molester, but a pervert to boot. Women's associations demanded a national boycott of Chaplin's films; there were demonstrations outside the studios; guards were placed on the buildings by the administrators; every coat hanger that a boy carried from A to B had to be registered; two of his Tramp costumes were confiscated.

Chaplin suffered a nervous breakdown, and couldn't speak for days. He interrupted work on *The Circus* for an indefinite period, every day of which cost United Artists a fortune. He withdrew from public life and moved into a hotel, abandoning his house on Summit Drive. The only people he had any contact with were the Fairbanks. The fact that Marion Davies invited Mr Charles Chaplin to the grand unveiling of her house was a statement. Douglas and Mary told him he mustn't reject such a declaration of sympathy.

Churchill had been invited by Hearst, not by Marion Davies; however, Hearst wasn't there – he and his mistress had argued that day. Churchill didn't know anyone personally, though he knew several of them by sight. He spent most of the party standing outside on the beach terrace by one of the pillars, his coat over his arm as if he was about to leave. Chaplin, worried that people would avoid him, also withdrew before they had a chance to, and came to stand by the next pillar along. A cold wind was blowing up from the Pacific. In the salon Edythe Baker, who was famous that season and was said to be unpredictably extravagant, started playing the piano, singing and dancing, and Chaplin and Churchill were soon the only ones left outside.

Churchill asked if Chaplin would care to accompany him on a walk along the beach. Chaplin pointed out that their smart party shoes would sink into the sand and get ruined, and they would end up with wet feet. Did that bother him, Churchill asked. It didn't bother him. On the contrary, said Chaplin, the very question lightened his heart.

They walked across the sand with their trousers rolled up, and came to the firm, damp strip at the water's edge, and as they headed north, parallel to the brightly-lit houses of Santa Monica Beach, Churchill asked: "Are you sick?"

"Do I look it?" Chaplin asked him in return.

"Yes."

"How do I look?"

"Like a man who is contemplating suicide," Churchill replied.

"You can't tell a thing like that in the dark."

"Is that so?"

On another occasion, one of them told the other he had decided at that moment not to introduce himself. Both found the prospect of an anonymous confession in the shadows of night more tempting than the idea of making the acquaintance of some celebrity or other. They admitted that although they may not have recognised the person they were talking to, they certainly recognised his personality, meaning that each recognised his own tribulations. Chaplin – who undoubtedly had an affinity with romantic archetypes – said that a shudder had run down his back at the thought of meeting a doppelganger (though admittedly this was a doppelganger who didn't resemble him in the slightest): a second self, clothed in the flesh of another, so to speak. Churchill – he too was deeply influenced by the 19th century's seductive flights of fancy (Bram Stoker, the author of *Dracula*, was a friend of his father's, and his very first speech, for an English exam at Harrow when he was fifteen, had been about Robert Louis Stevenson's novella *The Strange Case of Dr Jekyll and Mr Hyde*) – confirmed that similar thoughts had passed through his mind. The fact that he and Mr Chaplin differed so much – firstly in their appearance, secondly in their backgrounds, and thirdly and most importantly in their political views – made the whole business even more uncanny, but at the same time it also awoke in him a sense of familiarity he had never felt before.

"Is that so?" Churchill asked again.

"Yes, it is so," Chaplin replied.

5

A few months before his death, in summer 1977, Chaplin – who was now Sir Charles Chaplin – gave a long interview, the last he would give, to Josef Melzer, a journalist who had been commissioned by a German news magazine "to reveal the mystery of the silver screen's leading light, before he dissolved into light himself," as Melzer put it in the introduction to his book (*Chaplins Tugend* (Chaplin's Virtue), published by 'Amis' Verlag, Bern 1979). Alongside the correspondence between my father and William Knott, this book is the principal source for my own account. Melzer visited Chaplin at the Manoir de Ban, his villa in the vineyards above Vevey, which looked out onto Lake Geneva. Churchill had been dead for twelve years. Chaplin no longer felt bound by his scout's-honour oath, and granted Melzer an insight into the closely-guarded subject of this friendship, which all the world regarded as curious. He also spoke of their first encounter on Santa Monica Beach.

At first, he recalled, he had been afraid that the other man, whoever he might be, would recognise him and either turn away from him in disgust or offer his sympathy and solidarity, depending on which camp he fell into and which newspapers he read. His thoughts of suicide, as the stranger had correctly surmised, had become dangerously acute during the media witch-hunt of the preceding weeks, though the possibility had been with him ever since childhood. Under the starry sky of this Californian February night, he was once again faced with the appalling fact: though he'd had so many friends in his life, he had never once met somebody with whom he could have discussed this subject.

The stranger pointed at his wound. "Tell me about it," he said, "and I will listen."

"I was at a loss as to how and where to begin," Chaplin said into Josef Melzer's tape recorder. "A torrent of recollections flooded over me. Which is to say: certain recollections. It was as though there was a filter built into my memory, which let through only the recollections of my suicidal thoughts. I saw myself as a man who had now been floundering his way through life for thirty-eight years, doing everything he could to avoid hanging himself from the nearest tree or throwing himself off the nearest bridge or buying a pistol – which at that time would have been the easiest thing in the world – and putting a bullet in his head."

But, Melzer objected, even at such a moment he surely couldn't have forgotten that at that point, without any exaggeration, he was not only the most popular actor, but the most popular *person* in the world.

"Me?" Chaplin cried out, "Me? Do you mean that? Do you really mean that? What do you mean by that? I was nobody! It was all the Tramp! Everyone who recognised me in the street (and who not long before that would have been cheering me on), everyone saw me as the Tramp. The Tramp was loved. As if he and I were separate. As if he were someone else. A commentator wrote that there had to be a way of stopping me from playing the Tramp; I was no longer worthy of the role. Lita's lawyers checked whether they could apply for a restraining order on the character of the Tramp. Now that everyone was cursing me, they thought they could see my true self behind Charlie. They had invested in me, their love, their hopes, their *schadenfreude*, and now they felt betrayed. This stranger on Santa Monica beach, so I imagined, didn't care who I was. I thought he didn't know. I thought he saw in me neither Charlie the Tramp, nor Charles Spencer Chaplin the monster. I thought he had been sent to me from somewhere, and I wanted to tell him everything. But I didn't know how and where to begin without giving away my identity. We hadn't revealed much more than that we were both Englishmen."

And so he decided not to provide an account of his current tribulations, but to talk about their very beginnings – though that took no less effort.

"I..." he said, stopping and folding his arms tightly across his chest, and rocking back and forth to an imaginary rhythm, which was his custom when dictating the intertitles of a film to his secretary, "I am one of those rare people who at the age of six was already seriously contemplating departing this life voluntarily."

Churchill, who was afraid he'd catch cold if he didn't keep moving – as he told his private secretary William Knott fifteen years later – laid a hand on Chaplin's shoulder and gently pushed him forwards, a gesture that could also have been taken as sympathetic. Beyond the last houses, the world was black, and you couldn't see where the land ended and the water began. He thought that in the dark, his new friend would find it easier "to speak of the cliffs from which, as a child, he had gazed into that evil maw". He had decided his turn would come on the way back. He, too, wanted to tell his story. This was the dramatic structure he wanted to give their walk.

"I'm listening," he said, "and if you wish me to give my opinion, don't be ashamed to ask."

From Chaplin's account of this evening we know that he spoke about his mother, who had been a music hall soubrette and an occasional actress – "with a light complexion and violet eyes, and hair down to the backs of her knees".

He asked Churchill whether names like the London Pavilion meant anything in the circles he moved in – or the Alhambra, or the Poly Variety Theatre? Or the Canterbury Music Hall, or the Gatti Music Halls? He must surely know the Empire on Leicester Square?

"I'm sorry," Churchill replied.

"That's a shame. I thought perhaps your father might have visited one of these establishments at some point and told you about it.

Who knows, maybe it would have been one of my mother's performances. Or perhaps you might have been there yourself. That would have been a nice coincidence."

His father, he said, had also performed as a singer and an occasional impressionist. His parents had had a career before them that gave them something to boast about. His father used to inform anyone who would listen, and everyone else as well, that the only thing art was good for was to give the artist something to boast about. Because otherwise, he had nothing. Except brandy. And his father had too much of that in the end. The only wreath laid on his grave read "He died for his art".

His mother, Chaplin said, had brought him and his brother up on her own. Well, it wasn't so much a case of bringing them up than of bringing them along, from one rat-infested hole to the next, depositing them in orphanages in between.

And there was a colleague of his mother's, Eva Lester, known as "dashing Eva Lester", who had joined the troop in the Empire one day. She was beautiful, ruthless, ambitious. Chaplin's mother was moved to the second row, then the third, until she was just a reserve. Eventually she got out of show-business altogether. She felt the end of her career had been a disgrace, and thus would continually assure everyone that it was her own decision; from now on, she just wanted to take care of her two sons. They had no money. They were evicted, and ended up sub-letting a dank basement.

"But!" cried Chaplin. "But!"

"But?" said Churchill.

"But there is justice in the world!"

"Is that so?" He spoke with a hiss, making the words run into one another.

"Yes, that is so," said Chaplin.

Chaplin admitted that the way Churchill spoke had roused his urge to mimic him from the outset. This urge was an addiction he had now become conscious of. It had caused enough calamity in his life already; no matter what face he put on while he was being questioned by the divorce judge, the latter always felt he was being mimicked and mocked.

"One day, when I was..." – before uttering the next word, he told himself to be disciplined – "six years old, my mother took me to East Lane. To find something to eat. We met Eva Lester there. She wasn't dashing any longer, oh no. She was wretched. She was squatting on a corner, holding out a withered, dirty hand. She had cut off her hair, and her head was covered in scabby sores. She looked like an old woman, though she was younger than my mother. She said, well, it's nice to see *you've* made it, at least. Yes, said my mother, I've made it. Just imagine – my mother said that! She took Eva home to our basement. She washed her. She treated the scabs on her head. She rubbed cream into her and cooked for her. When she started to moan, my mother gave her some brandy she had inherited from my father."

Charlie's brother Sydney, who was older than him by four years, was working as a paper boy, and doing other odd jobs. He was out on the street all day – "the knight-errant of our welfare", as their mother called him. She earned a few shillings as a seamstress. But to do so she had to leave the house, since they didn't have their own sewing machine. Charlie was alone with Eva most of the time. She introduced him to life – that was what she called it.

"There is no store of happiness reserved for people like us," she said, "You know, little cherry eye, the most beautiful gift a person can receive is God's grace. And it's the only gift there is. Everything else is just titbits and treats, which are polished off in no time. If people are rich, that's proof they've been given God's grace. If they're beautiful and stay beautiful all their lives, and can buy a fancy suit every two years and go to a restaurant without squinting at the right-hand side of the menu before they order, then God's grace is on their side. And now look and me, and look at your mum. And look at you. What do we look like? You're as thin as a rake.

And let me tell you something else: whatever somebody can be, he is already. What do you want to be?"

He said he wanted to be an artist, like his father had been, like his mother was. And Eva explained to him what an artist was: a person who wanted to trick their way into God's grace; a person who'd got the knack of things, who'd figured out how it all worked.

"And how does it work?" Charlie asked apprehensively.

"I'll tell you. You, I'll tell, little cherry eye. But it's risky."

An artist, she said, deceived God in heaven. That's what art was, and nothing else. God's grace had given the artist talent, and what did he use it for? He portrayed a man on stage, and either made him better than he was, or worse. It was always a misrepresentation of God's work.

"And God in heaven doesn't notice?" asked Charlie.

"Oh, He does," said Eva. "He almost always notices."

"And what does God do when he notices?"

"He beats the artist up, that's what he does. Look at me. Look at your father. Look at your mum."

His heart still reverberated with the mighty tremor that Eva Lester's words had sent through him, the eighty-eight-year-old Chaplin confessed to Josef Melzer. All of a sudden, the world and the people in it appeared to him in a garish light – a place of misery full of miserable creatures, pushing and shoving and getting nowhere. There was nothing noble now in his father's demise, nothing noble in his mother's failure, nothing heroic in his brother's penny errands, no fore-glow of better days to come emanating from the little charcoal stove in their cellar – which they were only to light in the evenings, if possible. He was six years old, and he thought: I don't stand a chance.

"I was a smart little fellow, though, let me tell you," Chaplin said into Josef Melzer's microphone. "I thought I was capable of deceiving people. It would be a very difficult and a very wicked task, but I thought I could do it, and it didn't trouble my conscience too much. My father had always claimed that acting was deception, and he enjoyed pulling the wool over people's eyes. But he had never said that if you wanted to be a successful artist, you had to deceive God as well. He had reached the age of thirty-eight without knowing anything of this dubious honour. And I knew it at the age of six. Without having the words for it, I knew that if an artist failed, he would either end up miserable like Eva Lester, or a sly conformist, which was even worse, because there was no honour in it, because it meant you had given up trying (if not managing) to deceive God. But in most cases, artists lived and died poor and without honour, and were forgotten before a single weed had grown on their graves. This realisation sent a tremor right through me."

"What effect did that have on you as a child?" Josef Melzer asked. He was somewhat at a loss, because he thought he could detect a trace of that tremor in Chaplin's aged face, but he couldn't be sure it wasn't just an example of how an artist could deceive people – could deceive him, specifically.

Churchill asked a similar question on the beach in Santa Monica, though without the thought behind it. He was now convinced that walking in darkness had been exactly the right thing to do, the ocean drowning out the nuances of their words. He sensed his voice starting to quiver, and tears welling up in his eyes, and even if he had enough self-knowledge to judge that this was ninety per cent attributable to his own sentimental tendencies, the remaining ten per cent was enough to allow his hand to find that of the other man.

"That afternoon, I ran away," Chaplin replied. "I ran all the way to the Thames and over Tower Bridge, climbed a wall by the Pool and went hand-over-hand up the pegs of a wooden crane until I got to the top, ninety feet above the water. I sat astride the jib and wrestled with myself. Should I jump? Or shouldn't I? What could

I become if not an artist? I couldn't even consider any other profession, just as my father and mother could never have considered any other profession. And they didn't even manage to deceive the few dozen visitors to the Empire on Leicester Square. So how was I supposed to deceive God, who could see into your heart?"

They had been walking for a good hour, past Pacific Palisades with its smart beach houses, most of which lay in darkness, occupied only on summer weekends. They reached the point where the beach opened out and where, further inland, Sunset Boulevard joined the Pacific Coast Highway.

"That's enough," said Chaplin. "I've said what I wanted to say. Thank you. Let's go back."

"In that case, it's my turn," said Churchill.

6

He, too, was one of those rare people who at the age of six was already seriously contemplating departing this life voluntarily.

His father – that was where he began – had not been proud of him. He'd had no reason to be proud of him.

Until his sixth year, he had been a happy child. His parents were abroad, and he was looked after by a nanny. "Brought up" would have been overstating it. The woman never asked herself what this child might become. His family was unsinkable. Added to which he owned a fleet of ships, a thousand tin soldiers, a magic lantern and a steam engine that came with a dozen working models both large and small, among them a brewery, a saw mill, a smithy, a dockyard, a cobbler's workshop and even an electricity plant. Heating the machine up to full power took half a day, and arranging the soldiers into battle formation took a whole day. In the evenings he fell asleep with the feeling that he had done something worthwhile. He was never again praised so fulsomely and so imaginatively as he was by his nanny, Mrs Everest. Until his sixth year, he believed he was the most intelligent child on earth. He didn't think of his activities as games, but work, no less valuable than the work his father did, about which all he knew was that it was of great significance for the British Empire.

His parents returned, and he had them all to himself for precisely two weeks before they packed him off to boarding school. And after two weeks there, he knew he wasn't the most intelligent child on earth, but the stupidest.

He was homesick for Mrs Everest; he missed her resolute way of spreading butter on bread and plumping up the pillows, her *schadenfreude* when the dog chased his own tail; he longed for her astonished face when he showed her the things he'd built, and for her martial exclamations when he told her how the British fleet under Admiral Nelson had defeated the French and the Spanish at Trafalgar. Mrs Everest would whoop and cheer as if it had only just happened. And it *had* only just happened; he was inside Nelson's skin. "*I* unleashed a salvo which smashed the enemy's ships and made him start to waver," he said, reworking the words Mrs Everest had read to him from a children's history book that he had learned off by heart. What magic, what a delight – he just had to turn "he" into "I" and he was right in the middle of things: he, Winston Leonard Churchill! *He* was giving the orders, *he* was thinking up strategies, *he* stood on the bridge of the HMS Victory and looked across the sea at the enemy armada; the king made *him* a viscount. And Mrs Everest provided an accompanying fanfare of curses so loud it could be heard out in the garden. She cursed Napoleon: "Dimwit! Know-it-all! Dunderhead!" She cursed the Spanish Admiral Pierre de Villeneuve: "Arse-licker! Filthy swine! Coward!" But her loudest and coarsest curses were reserved for the French fusilier who had fired the fatal shot at Nelson from the mizzen of the *Redoutable* – "Go to hell, you damned bastard!" All of these expressions, she explained to her young charge once she had cooled off a little, could be used in front of his parents with a clear conscience – if the conversation was to turn to Napoleon. In this case, he might even earn praise. Other phrases from her repertoire, such as "I'll have your guts for garters", he would do better to keep to himself, along with her favourite term for everything that confounded her will and her ideas: "Brewed yellow shit!"

Mrs Everest was very proud of her darling boy. The idea that he would become the stupidest pupil the venerable St James's School had ever admitted – well, she would have bet her life against such a prophecy.

The headmaster couldn't believe what his teachers were telling him, either. He refused to believe that a boy of this pedigree didn't know the answer to a single question. He couldn't believe that after nine months of instruction the boy was still drawing lines on his slate where letters and numbers should have been.

At the start of the new school year, he summoned the boy and placed a piece of paper in front of him. On it was written:

Mensa: a table
Mensa: O table
Mensam: a table
Mensae: of a table
Mensae: to or for a table
Mensa: by, with or from a table

He was to learn this by heart and think up some examples. He had half an hour.

Winston considered the task, and wrote:

There is <u>a table</u> in the room.
A plate is on top <u>of a table</u>
I take a vase <u>to a table</u>
<u>With a table</u> I barricade the door.

He didn't know what *O table* meant.

"It's the vocative case," the headmaster explained. "Don't you know what the vocative is?"

"No."

"You would use the vocative in conversation with a table. If you were talking to a table, or addressing it, for example: *O table, stay where you are!* Then you would have to use the vocative."

"But I don't talk to tables," he said, "especially not if they're moving about."

"On the contrary," the headmaster insisted. "If you want to learn Latin declensions, you will have to bring yourself to talk to tables, even if they move about."

"But I don't want to."

"You must! In this school, you must."

The anecdote is well known. Churchill recounted it in his book *My Early Life*; there is no biography of the statesman that fails to quote it.

The incident is depicted in the book as something truly British and absurdly humorous, but in truth it robbed the six-year-old Winston of his peace of mind. He thought: I'm not in school. This isn't a school. This is a madhouse. They speak to walking tables here.

His longing for Mrs Everest burned inside him. He longed for her praise, her enthusiasm, and her curses; he saw her in his mind's eye, running alongside the hansom cab with her skirts hitched up, begging his father not to do this to her darling boy, and he saw his father laughing under his handlebar moustache and calling out to her through the window of the cab that for pity's sake, St James's School wasn't the Tower, and his son wasn't Edward V. And now finally he felt certain that the headmaster and the teachers of this school weren't the only lunatics; his father and, who knew, maybe even his mother (who had merely smiled) were also among them. In truth, the whole Empire, with the exception of himself and Mrs Everest, was mad. How else could his father be such an important person, and St James's such a renowned school?

What happened next was something Churchill omitted from his memoir. He had never spoken of it to anyone: not to Mrs Everest, or his parents, and not to his wife. But he wanted to tell the stranger on the beach in Santa Monica.

He was still standing in the headmaster's office, he said. The walls were clad in a dark-coloured wood, and at the centre of the room stood the desk that all the boys were afraid of: nothing good had ever come of having to stand before this desk. The headmaster was already at the door, with his hand on the handle, meaning the interview was at an end and he, the pupil, was now permitted to go back to class. But he didn't budge an inch. In his mind's eye, Churchill told the stranger, he had seen Mrs Everest, running alongside the cab and pleading with his father until she could run no further. And suddenly he felt as though someone else was rising up inside him, someone much bigger, a scoundrel, a drinker, a master of the cutting remark, a hero of disrepute with a laugh like the man who sometimes visited Mrs Everest at night, and whom he had heard, but never seen. And then it came bursting out. He had taken note of Mrs Everest's curses, the bad ones in particular, he had forgotten none of them – this was vocabulary he *had* learned. A voice he didn't recognise, which sounded to his ears like an adult's voice, an unhurried, unflustered voice, almost without passion, pronounced one curse after another to the headmaster's face.

The headmaster was so shocked he couldn't think. He could think of nothing to say, he could think of nothing to do. So he said and did nothing.

That same night, Churchill continued, he had slipped out of the dormitory, climbed out of a window in the corridor and shinned down a drainpipe from the first floor into the schoolyard. The school was surrounded by a wall which the headmaster made a point of showing the boys on their first day, to quash all hopes of escape. The wall was five metres high and topped with iron spikes, which looked decorative but were actually razor sharp, as the headmaster had told them with a smug little smile. He didn't know what to do. But he didn't want to go back to the dormitory. He didn't want to talk to anyone. He never wanted to speak to another person again. He crept along the side of the school building, so he couldn't be seen from inside. He was barefoot and wearing nothing but a nightshirt. He fell down the coal hole, banged his head and thought he had died. It took him a while to orient himself. The window of the cellar was no bigger than his satchel. There was a piece of cloth hanging across it. He squeezed through and rolled down a ramp onto a heap of coal. He felt for a way out of the coal cellar and found a light switch. Somewhere, a bulb came on. He went from one cellar room to the next, through larders and wine stores, past lumber rooms and detention rooms. Eventually he found himself in front of a locked iron door, although the key was still in the lock. He opened the door and entered a narrow room that housed the main switch and the fuse box for the school's electricity supply. This was something he knew about. A similar system in miniature had come with his steam engine, along with a small turbine that turned the steam pressure into electricity. The main switch was a Y-shaped lever. The current flowed through the two arms. The cables underneath were exposed. Giving in to an impulse, he placed his hand on the copper wire. He was thrown back through the door. The electricity was cut off throughout the building.

He was discovered unconscious, with burns on his hand and forearm. The school decided not to inform his parents. The headmaster and the teachers were confident that Winston wouldn't say anything about it himself. They knew the children were more afraid of their parents than of their teachers. He spent two weeks in the infirmary, being served meals from the teachers' table. The other boys were told he had a sort of flu that produced a rash on the arms, and was very infectious.

When they got back to Marion Davies's beach house, it was long past midnight. Most of the guests had slipped away, not wanting to have their names connected with the mysterious disappearance of a prominent film star and a no less prominent politician. The decent types, among them the Fairbanks, of course, had begun to search for them, phoning friends and looking in nearby bars and restaurants. Everyone refused to believe that the pair would have left the party without saying goodbye to the hostess. And nobody had hit upon the idea that they might just have gone for a walk on the beach. Miss Davies had wanted to call the police, but was prevented by "Mr Brown", one of Hearst's henchmen.

"William Randolph would stop at nothing to prevent his name being linked to a scandal," she said, adding twice as loudly: "Even if that meant Winston and Charlie perished as a result." She was known for her savage way of embellishing the truth.

But neither savagery nor truth could daunt the pair. They had told one another of the times they had been bowed by powers that were not of this world. And the troubles that had weighed heavy at the start of their walk now felt a little lighter.

7

That night, Chaplin slept in his office at the studio. He took a long shower, and at nine o'clock he asked Miss Nicolaisen to fry him a steak, before facing his correspondence, the newspapers, the day. The articles in the press had become less hate-filled, and had slipped from the front page to the second and then the third; the hate mail and threatening letters could now be brought to the office in Mrs Pryor's hands, rather than in baskets – but there was still enough to despair over.

It was by no means certain that *The Circus* would ever be finished. The idea that this work might founder was very painful to him. He thought it his best. If he was going to order his work according to the life story of the Tramp, rather than chronologically, then this adventure would come first. The Tramp could pop up anywhere, in any randomly chosen city, in the countryside, in the Alaskan wilderness, on an ocean-going steamer, even in the Wild West – but his real home was the travelling show, the circus ring. People had always asked: where did he come from, when he arrived; where did he go to, when he went? Why didn't he stay? Here was the answer. He felt he had never come closer to his own "poetic truth". A journalist – from the time when journalists were still well-disposed towards him – had coined this phrase in an interview after the premiere of *The Kid*. Chaplin hadn't understood what he meant by it. The Tramp had always been a puzzle to him; he didn't know who this fellow really was. He had no backstory, and he hadn't developed over the course of his appearances, in the way that comic characters usually do – like Harold Lloyd's bookkeeper type, W.C. Fields's misanthrope, the crossed-eyed smart aleck Ben Turpin and other colleagues from the Keystone Studios days; he didn't reference any tradition, he wasn't a Harlequin, a Pierrot, he wasn't an Auguste, and he certainly wasn't a whiteface; he had just appeared one day, complete, unknown, puzzling. He revealed more of himself for the first time in *The Circus*; he wasn't a stranger there. Even if he makes the audience laugh by doing everything wrong, we sense that he knows very well – better than his inventor does – that in this place, the wrong thing is the right thing. When Chaplin saw the first rushes, he went into raptures over the pantomime, which revealed so much more than he had intended while performing it, and with a shudder he had told Roland Totheroh, who was behind the camera once again, that he had finally realised something: he didn't control the Tramp; the Tramp controlled him. And Roland had nodded reverently. Now he thought he understood what was meant by "poetic truth".

But the break in production saw the film's costs rise to unprofitable levels. And fiasco, debacle and screw-ups continued to dog them: the rushes were spoiled, with scratches "of a mysterious origin", as Tim O'Donnell, the head of the laboratory, put it. Chaplin had the whole technical team replaced. A fire brought business at the studio to a halt for weeks – the cause of the catastrophe: "mysterious". With the exception of the main supporting actors and Merna Kennedy, the female lead, the ensemble had to be dismissed. Which led to threats of legal action. And to heartrending scenes. Betty Morrissey, who was only twenty – she played the magician's assistant – offered up her own suicide to shame their enemies and prompt a turn-around; the boss, she later said, had been the only one who could see she wasn't joking. On top of this, Chaplin was suffering from a chronic stomach complaint, for which his physician, Dr Van Riemsdyk, had prescribed Epsom salts, leading to continual belching and diarrhoea, and dangerous weight loss. And the IRS had him in their sights. They were of the opinion that Mr Charles Chaplin owed $1,113,000 in income tax. He finally settled on a million with them, after which a lawsuit for tax evasion was dropped. (For comparison: two years previously, the filming of *Ben Hur* by Metro-Goldwyn-Mayer, which at that point was the most monumental production in the history of cinema, had cost four million dollars.) At the same time the courts ruled that he had to pay Lita $600,000, plus $200,000 for their two sons. Chaplin's legal costs ran to another million.

Sydney Chaplin, the managing director of United Artists, who at this time was living in New York and weighing up the advantages and disadvantages of moving the studios to the East Coast, wrote to his brother: "I do hate to paint GLOOM but it does seem to me that we should be prepared to go to the other side" (he meant back to England). And then he did paint GLOOM after all: "When I am feeling sort of worried, myself, I always think of the great joy, happiness and elated feeling I had when I signed on the dotted line for Fred Karno [the director of the touring company in which they played their first roles as boys] – just think, the great sum of three pounds a week – why I ran all the way to Kennington Road to send you the glad news. So it seems, after all, that happiness is a matter of comparison." Sydney knew the company's books like nobody else; he knew United Artists was hanging by a brittle thread over the abyss – much like the prospectors' hut in *The Gold Rush*. He could hear people drawing breath for a final great laugh at their expense.

At midday, a messenger arrived with a letter. Mr Winston Churchill invited Mr Charles Chaplin to dinner at the Biltmore Hotel on Pershing Square, where he was staying with his wife and daughter. There was a P.S. on the card: "Please, <u>don't</u> bring anyone else."

Chaplin phoned his brother and reported the news.

"Go," said Sydney. "He's an illustrious man. He holds the British Empire's purse strings. If we really did have to move back, he could help us. He's obviously crazy about you, which is a good thing. Tell him you feel the call of home, or something like that. Just don't tell him about our situation. Men like him have no time for losers.

England should be glad to have us back. That's how it should look. Say something like that, a hint or a bit more than a hint, you're good at that. Maybe you can also mention, just in passing of course, that we're British citizens, we never became Americans, and we've still got our British passports. Will you?"

"Yes, I will."

"Promise me!"

"Yes, I promise."

He wouldn't be able to explain to his brother what he and His Majesty's Chancellor of the Exchequer had talked about the previous night on Santa Monica beach, or that it hadn't mattered that one of them was the Chancellor of the Exchequer and the other was a film artist, or whether either of them would remain so, or for how long.

He was looking forward to the evening...

8

...which then began so disappointingly.

They were seated in a booth at the back of the dining room; only an impolite manoeuvre would afford someone a view of their table. It was unlikely that the other guests understood what Churchill, speaking in a high-pitched stage whisper, meant by his plan for a "future alliance against the black dog"; but Chaplin could hear that they were drawing everyone's attention, because during the few pauses in his companion's speech he could hear nothing, where normally there would be voices, laughter, the clatter of cutlery. He was certain that by now, everyone in the room knew who was dining back there – that had clearly been taken care of. Hollywood's waiters and waitresses didn't just earn their living by serving cocktails and steaks, but also by passing on rumours.

Chaplin said he remembered feeling very uncomfortable. He was bothered – repelled, in fact – by Churchill's all-round ebullience, and even more repelled by his immoderate consumption of alcohol and nicotine. He had the impression that Churchill wasn't raising his glass to give emphasis to his speech; he was speaking in order to raise his glass. And when he spoke, smoke billowed from his mouth as if his belly were a charcoal kiln. The only way he could tolerate this forced joviality was by squinting in order to obliterate the scene.

"And so, let us promise one another that, whenever one of us requires aid in this battle, the other, wherever in the world he may be, will drop everything to assist him!"

It felt, said Chaplin, like Churchill was performing for him. His voice was louder than necessary, much louder. As if he wanted people to listen. He was trying to demonstrate to the world that in spite of all its malevolence, Mr Charles Chaplin had not forgotten how to have a good time. But Mr Charles Chaplin didn't want to demonstrate anything to anyone.

He had been offended, Josef Melzer commented. In Chaplin's view, the significance he had attached to their night-time stroll was not something to be made into a public statement, or treated ironically. Now it seemed to him that Churchill was intent on both; above all he intended to make light of it, in that masculine fashion that was customary in English gentlemen's clubs, with ceremonies consisting of nonsense and drinking. It all seemed very childish to him – the "black dog"! He had never seen any animalistic quality in his depression, and it certainly wasn't a dog – why not a teddy bear, come to that? He had owned a black dog years ago, a miniature schnauzer that had come up to him while they were filming *A Woman of Paris*, and waited for him every evening on the corner of Hollywood Boulevard and Cherokee Street. He took it to Henry's and had the Filipino chef there chop up a rump steak for it, a very dear animal that no one had been afraid of, not even the postman.

And so he gave quite a fatuous response: "I couldn't say what colour my mood was, if it was any colour at all, and if it really was an animal, which is an idea I find both sentimental and spine-chilling, then I would rather..."

"I'm an imperialist," Churchill barked at him, now very serious and sober, "a John Bull. I'm like England. I force my ideas on the whole world. I admire Samuel Johnson, though I haven't read more than five pages of him. But they were the five pages in which he described his illness, and I thought he was talking about me. That was enough to give me a good opinion of him. He called his illness 'the black dog'. Why should we come up with a new name?"

If Chaplin had told his friends thirty years earlier that one day he would be drinking champagne with this gentleman in an upmarket hotel in Los Angeles, they'd have given him a kicking for being big-headed. Of course, Churchill was an illustrious man, but back then he had been a legend, a mythical figure. The crowds had cheered him in Trafalgar Square, and at ten years old Charlie had pushed his way through the throng to stare at him close-up. His small, undernourished frame made that easier for him than it was for the other children. There wasn't a single person in the British Empire who didn't know this man's story, a heroic tale that might have been written by Walter Scott: taken prisoner in the Boer War, he had escaped in spectacular fashion, and wandered for days across the Karoo Desert with nothing more than a half-full canteen of water, a melting bar of Cadbury's chocolate and a scrap of parachute silk. He had finally dug himself into the coal heap aboard a freight train and stayed put until he arrived in neutral Mozambique, black as a Zulu. He returned home in triumph, with a great future ahead of him. He had grown thin, and his hair was long and wavy and combed back in a dashing style.

And now he was sitting opposite this former incarnation of Ivanhoe, pretending to listen – and finding even that difficult. Churchill kept getting up out of his seat, his eyes darting about. He talked and gesticulated. And hissed. And worked himself into a pathos that made the air in their booth heavy. What am I doing here? Chaplin wondered. He had lost every trace of that night-time magic. A doppelganger? Absurd! He looked into the coarse, puffy face. A picture puzzle in which you could see a baby or an old man, not the face of an aristocratic gentleman. No matter how conscientious his grooming, Churchill would always look unkempt. His suit fitted badly. Any suit would look terrible on this man – just as any suit would look good on Chaplin.

Sometimes Chaplin would distribute flyers in the city, or put an ad in one of the newspapers to say that the Chaplin Studios were looking for an actor or an actress. People would line up outside. He'd say: Act out who you are! I don't want to see Juliet or Othello, I'd like to see you! And with a clandestine delight he would watch

one after another of them grow flustered. Then *he* would act out
who they were. They all recognised themselves, with as little doubt
as if they were looking in a mirror. And they were shaken to the
core. Very few were angry; most were grateful and shook his hand,
even after he had told them they weren't needed.

He couldn't imitate absolutely anyone – his friends and his
enemies all claimed he could, but that wasn't true – though some
he could do without a second thought, simply letting his muscles
and tendons take over. Others, however, were completely foreign to
him and remained so. It would be easy to imitate Mr Churchill. He
would play him so true to life that anyone in the viewing room or
looking up at the screen would be able to see past the thick, dark,
curly hair and imagine a bald head with a sparse, reddish-blonde
comb-over. His svelte, lithe body would show plumpness more
convincingly than plumpness itself, and, if he wanted, the interplay
of nose and mouth, frown lines and Adam's apple, eyebrows and
chin would yield an insight into the depths of his heart – which he
would not model on any preconception, but would only discover
himself in the course of his performance.

"What do you think?" Churchill said, interrupting his train of
thought. "Say something! This isn't just about me. It's about you,
too. That's the essence of an alliance!"

He didn't know what to think, or what he was supposed to be
thinking about. He hadn't been listening.

Churchill's drunken state fuelled the pathos in his speech, but it
didn't dampen his perceptiveness or dull his sensitivity. He stood
motionless, looking past Chaplin. He had not been listened to. He
had been proselytising into the smoke from his own cigar. He stood
motionless, staring at the silk wallpaper above Chaplin's parting.
He might have flown into a rage; he might have made the error
of reflecting on the differences between his guest's background
and his own; he might have struck a certain tone and chosen
certain words – it hadn't happened often, but the few times it had,

it had destroyed his relationship with certain people forever. (In his memoirs Brendan Bracken, a good friend of the Churchills', mentions an awful outburst from Winston after a speech during which members of his own faction had done crossword puzzles, filed their nails and made paper boats. "Had they criticised him and torn his speech apart, had they mocked him, even, he would have forgiven them, but he could not forgive their inattention.") Perhaps the newly germinated friendship between Charlie Chaplin and Winston Churchill would have died again – if at that moment the head waiter hadn't appeared, holding a young girl by the hand: Sarah, Churchill's daughter, thirteen years old.

She couldn't sleep, she said, resting her head of coppery hair against her father's arm. She was barefoot and wearing a turquoise night-dress; she had a long, narrow face and very white teeth. Could she sit with them, she asked. She called her father "Pomp". She greeted Chaplin with a nod. She knew who he was, she said. He was the most famous man in the world. She had seen all his films.

Churchill changed in an instant. The rest of the evening he drank no more alcohol. The colour in his face settled into an even pink. His voice became deep and soft, his gestures generous. He smiled and held their gaze. Never in his life had he encountered a more affectionate father, Chaplin said. And never a more affection-ate daughter.

"Mr Chaplin can mimic anyone in the world," said Churchill.

"Mimic how?"

"So that you would recognise him straight away."

"Absolutely anyone?"

"Absolutely."

"I don't believe it."

He had found it uncanny, Chaplin said, and his laughter could be heard for a long time on Josef Melzer's tape, until Melzer started laughing as well. As if, he said, growing serious again – as if his thoughts had remained hanging in the air, visible only to this girl. Sarah said: "Has he ever done you, Pomp? I'm sure he couldn't do you – not *you*."

"Don't you think so?" Churchill said. "Shall we ask him to try?"

"Yes," she cried. "Let's ask him!"

"I believe she saw through us," Chaplin said fifty years later. "When she looked at me, which she did without any embarrassment, I felt she knew about both of us. About us cripples." (Another long laugh) – "She was afraid for her father. And I think she was a little afraid for me, too, because I was the only one who could help her father."

This fearfulness in her eyes had brought her father back into his heart.

Chaplin was ashamed of his rebelliousness and his inattention. And of his plebeian arrogance. He was ashamed to have placed so little trust in his friend. People could say what they liked about Chaplin – it wouldn't matter to Churchill. If he really was the abominable cad that Lita and her lawyers and the conniving journalists kept telling the world he was, it wouldn't matter to Churchill. Politically, they were diametrically opposed: one of them saw Ghandi as an insignificant naked Fakir, while the other saw him as a great politician who could do a great deal for the British Empire; one of them trusted in Communism to abolish injustice, while the other described it as a machine for the equal sharing of miseries; one of them had, just a year previously, called for the British workers' general strike to be crushed by force, while the other sent a telegram from the US to express his solidarity with the unions; one of them was His Majesty's Chancellor of the Exchequer, and the other the most famous actor in the history of acting – but none of this mattered. They had a common enemy within them. Their enemy wasn't lurking in the chic, gold and vanilla dining room of the Biltmore Hotel, or in scandal-hungry Hollywood, or in the brains of a bunch of sleazy writers, or in the lawyers' offices or behind the judges' benches. He wasn't lurking in some party headquarters, or in the trenches beyond the barbed wire – he was within them, and this enemy was the reason for their alliance. Everything else was off limits, and would never be discussed.

When they bade each other farewell, he said to Churchill: "Let us promise each other that, whenever one of us is in need of aid, the other, no matter where in the world he is, will drop everything to assist him!"

He put out his hand and suggested they call each other Winston and Charlie. And Churchill – who had started to weep again – agreed.

9

Not long after this, they took a walk together into the Malibu Hills. Once again, it was Churchill who made the suggestion. The festivities were over, he said on the telephone, and now the matter must be addressed in a sober fashion. It was time to compare methods, and perhaps to develop new ones.

"Why the Malibu Hills?" asked Chaplin.

"There's something I want to show you."

Churchill and his chauffeur were waiting outside a Mexican restaurant on the Pacific Coast Highway. He had a rucksack packed with tacos and water bottles, and some chocolate. No alcohol. He was wearing sturdy shoes, a windproof cape and a leather hat. He had a machete in a linen bag. He wanted to carry everything himself; he didn't hand anything over. Chaplin had envisaged a gentle stroll, and was wearing a white suit and white slip-on shoes. He had brought no provisions.

The chauffeur drove them into the hills. Where the track became too stony for the Dodge, Churchill told him to pull over. He should wait three hours before starting to worry, he said. It was midday, and the sun was beating down, but the air was cool and the breeze blowing off the Pacific grew stronger the higher they climbed. Churchill went ahead; soon he started panting, and soon he had to rest. He was sweating, his face was blotchy, and so was his shirt. Chaplin was not sweating. As far as he was concerned, he said, they could just sit down on the sand, perhaps in the shade of a bush. It all looked exactly the same up there as it did down here; there was nothing new up ahead. Churchill shook his head and walked on. Chaplin let him lead the way. There was no track here, just a narrow path, made either by people or animals. It was hard going, overgrown in places, and deep furrows gaped beneath the branches and twigs where the rain had washed away the soil. It would be easy to slip and break an ankle. Churchill unwrapped the linen from around the machete and started hacking at the undergrowth. Had he been here before, Chaplin asked. No, not here – he had seen pictures, photographs. He stopped, unable to go on speaking.

"Give me the machete – I'll go first," said Chaplin.

Churchill refused. He was looking for a particular place. He would know when he'd found it. When he had got his breath back, he said they had to be aware that they were at the end of the West. They looked down at the semi-circle of the Pacific, its far edge merging with the sky in a blue and white haze. Could he manage another few yards, Churchill asked. *Me,* cried Chaplin, could *I* manage? He asked Churchill at least to give him the rucksack. He was looking for a particular place, Churchill repeated, shouldering the rucksack and the machete and setting off again.

Before long, he stopped again and sat down heavily on the ground.

"It's not here," he said.

"What is this place you're looking for?" Chaplin asked. "Everything looks the same here, believe me."

"A place to paint," said Churchill. "A place where I would set up my easel if I had come here to paint."

He painted. That was his method. On canvas. Oil on canvas. Landscapes, mainly. Occasionally portraits. A landscape didn't talk when it was modelling for you. Landscapes had been what they were long before he arrived, and would remain so long after he had gone. The same went for the sky. Painting people didn't particularly interest him.

"What colour is the sky? Everyone says it's blue. And it is, isn't it? Look at the sky, Charlie! Is it blue? And so the painter mixes a blue and compares it to the sky, but it's quite different. He makes a new mixture, he adds some yellow, he tries again, puts in a dab of violet. It's not right. He tries getting to blue via green. That doesn't work either. He starts with white, and the sky looks dull, as if it's made of stoneware. He tries again and again. And never pulls it off. In Milton, Adam has hyacinth-coloured locks, and so does Homer's Odysseus. But neither Homer nor Milton was mad. That's what I think about. It's a wonderful distraction, believe you me. I don't have anything more to offer. I'm afraid I have nothing better to offer. But that's alright."

"That's why you brought me up here," said Chaplin. It wasn't a question. It sounded like praise.

"I would sit here like this," said Churchill, straightening his back. "That's how I sit when I paint. I would hold the palette in one hand, and the brush in the other. I would tie my hat under my chin. I thought if you saw it, you might understand. You're thinking we might have spared ourselves this arduous walk. But I can't simply say: I paint. And that's that. I thought that if you saw it, you would understand."

"I understand, Winston," said Chaplin. "When he's there, the black dog, then..." All he could think to say was: "...then...it's bad, Winston, am I right?" He couldn't find any more elegant words for it, he told Josef Melzer. But he had never met anybody who could think of an elegant word on this subject.

They sat there, side by side, for a long time. Churchill, as if he were painting. Chaplin, as if he were watching him paint. Below them were pines and blossom-speckled cacti. Joshua trees stabbed the sky, unbending in the wind, like skeletons after a fire. Birds flocked around the treetops, picking seeds from them, their cries floating up to the two men. They had moved closer to a bush, to shield themselves from the wind. They were enveloped in the sour smell of the sagebrush, which killed off everything else wherever it grew. Chaplin had let the wild sage keep growing at the back of his garden; sometimes he sawed off branches to burn in his stove.

Finally Churchill said: "I'm hungry, and I'd like to smoke." They unpacked the rucksack, ate the tacos, drank water from the bottles, and chatted about this and that. Churchill lit a cigar in the shelter of his jacket. He left the chocolate for Chaplin.

After a while he asked: "And what's your method, Charlie?"

And Chaplin replied: "The method of the clown."

I am exploiting Josef Melzer's book here to an unfair degree. But truth be told, no other source is nearly as compact nor as rich as *Chaplin's Virtue* – neither Geoffrey Power's commendable anthology of Chaplin's statements to the press, nor Erica Southern's *Interview With the Tramp* – and in any case, there is no reason to disbelieve Pierre Kessler, the maestro's French secretary, when he claimed that Chaplin himself saw Melzer's book as his legacy. The book went through two editions, though it has long been out of print, and the publishing house no longer exists; the central association of antiquarian booksellers on the internet, as I discovered at the start of my work, only had three copies for sale.

Josef Melzer says that at this point in his interview, Chaplin got up from his basket chair and played out his recollections of that afternoon in the Malibu Hills. First he was Chaplin, then Churchill. First he was himself at the age of thirty-eight, seeming no less supple than he had been back then. What a masterful piece of acting! Then he was Churchill. By magic, "ancient magic", he summoned him from beyond the grave, this man who was so wholly different from him, and brought him to the spring garden of the Manoir de Ban above Vevey. He talked like Churchill, moved like Churchill, fell silent and thought like Churchill; he hissed and stuck out his lower lip to one side; and for the duration of the performance Melzer said he was conscious that in this man, he saw before him "the prototype from which the Almighty created all possible men throughout eternity".

Chaplin began with a rhetorical question: "Why is a clown a clown? There's nothing funny about him. The greatest clown is Buster Keaton. What's so funny about Buster Keaton? What makes him a clown? The knowledge that the world is *meschugge*? Humans are as small as fleas. But the spirit of a flea, so the poets tell us, is unnaturally wicked."

And Churchill said: "No foreword, please! The method, Charlie! No theory! We're only interested in practice!"

"Alright. The practice. I write a letter to myself. Understand, Winston? A letter to myself."

"I don't understand."

"Buster Keaton put me onto the method. I should get myself a large sheet of paper, he said. And I should lay it out on the floor. See?"

"Yes. Go on, Charlie, go on!"

"I lie down on this sheet of paper."

"How?"

"Face down."

"Face down, all right. Go on, go on!"

"I lie on this paper like a meal on a tablecloth. Are you laughing at me, Winston?"

"No, Charlie. Am I laughing? Look at me! Am I laughing? Is that laughter? That's not laughter. That's just how my face is."

"The only remedy for the thought that I might be mad is to do something mad. This is very serious, Winston. This is the method of the clown. There is no man in the world more serious than a clown."

"Yes, yes, I understand. I've read as much, a hundred times over. Go on!"

"I have to be naked. I can't have anything to do with the world. I have to be alone with myself. That's very important. Even a pair of trousers is the world, and a shirt is the world, too."

"You're right about that."

"I lie on the paper and write a letter. Please, Winston, don't laugh. Are you laughing? No, you're not laughing. I write a letter to myself. Dear Charlie, I write, and I write whatever comes into my head. If you try this method, don't give into the temptation to write to a friend. To me, for example. You mustn't write Dear Charlie. Write: Dear Winston. You're certain to think of the right thing to say, don't worry about that. Because at that moment everything is right and everything is important."

"I'll take that to heart."

"But listen, I don't write in the way one usually writes."

"Then how?"

"As I write, I turn."

"How do you turn?"

"Like the hand of a clock. I turn on my belly. As I write."

"Writing in a circle. A letter to oneself."

"In a spiral, to be exact. Working inwards. It's like a maelstrom. That's how it should be."

"That's how it should be. Like a maelstrom. Yes. Go on!"

"That's all. That really is all, Winston."

"Has it helped?"

"Yes."

After a very long silence – so Chaplin told Josef Melzer – they got up and carried on walking, up to the highest point of the hill. There, Churchill said: "You are a commander, Charlie. As clear-sighted as Wallenstein, as spirited as Nelson, as merciless as Arminius. I would like to learn from you. May I learn from you? How large is the sheet of paper? An exact measurement, please! Length? Breadth?

"Five and a half feet. And as wide as it is long. That's the best way; then you can turn comfortably in a circle on it."

"And what do you write with: a fountain pen, a pencil, chalk?"

"Ah, I've never thought about that. Anything that comes to hand."

"You mean any weapon will do?"

"Any weapon to strike at the beast – indeed, Winston!"

"You are a commander, Charlie," Churchill repeated. The pale blue Pacific was at his back, the island of Santa Catalina a silhouette on the southern horizon, as he stood with legs apart, the machete in one hand, a cigar in the other, trouser legs and cape flapping in the breeze, red-faced, sweating, panting – thus he stood, in the shadows of the late afternoon. "You've found a good method, Charlie. I think there is no better one for you."

10

In September, Chaplin started work on *The Circus* again after an eight-month hiatus.

Sydney said: "While everyone was hanging their heads and the corners of their mouths were drooping further and further with each piece of bad news, you could hear Charlie singing a mile off, and when he walked through the door, he would sashay like Bill Bojangles Robinson. Most people thought his troubles had finally driven him crazy. But they were still happy to see him."

In October, Alan Crosland's *The Jazz Singer*, with the Broadway star Al Jolson in the title role, was shown to a select audience. It was hailed as the first sound film, and was certainly the first talkie – Chaplin would later insist doggedly on this distinction. He was invited to the premiere in New York, but he didn't go, not wanting to interrupt his work on *The Circus* "even for a single hour". He was unsettled by reports of its incredible success, but not for long. He welcomed technological innovations that enabled a director to stipulate once and for all what music should accompany his images. In this respect, United Artists was limping along behind Warner Brothers. But in Chaplin's studio, too, people were starting to take these developments very seriously. A young freelancer, Artie G. Milford, was experimenting with something called the sound-on-disc system, and with the Vitaphone system, in which the film projector was coupled to a record player – labour-intensive and liable to fail; not very satisfactory – but Artie was also tinkering around with his own ideas. For *A Woman in Paris* and *The Gold Rush*, Chaplin had composed melodies and given them to an arranger, and at the original screenings they were played by an orchestra. He thought the director should be responsible for the music, either relying on a composer, or composing it himself. In short: music, yes; words, no. There was no future for the spoken word on screen – that was so obvious to him that he didn't even consider taking a stand to defend pantomime (people only started talking about "silent films" long after the invention of the talkie). When the starving, desperate Tramp cooked and ate his dirty boot, serving it up with perfect table manners, first lifting off the upper to leave the sole lying there with its skeleton of nails, like the ribs of a fish from which the fillet has been removed – when, before eating the leather, he licked the nails clean like chicken bones and twirled the laces around his fork like spaghetti, he was understood just as well in Japan as he was in the Congo. He was understood by the Laplanders in Scandinavia and the Aborigines in Australia. If you wanted to translate this scene into words and explain it with words, you'd have to write a bloody long, bloody clever book.

A month after the premier of the first sound film, *The Circus* – Chaplin's last "pure" silent film – was complete. It was 19 November 1927. That night the producer, director, screenwriter, cutter, principal actor – and later the composer of the film music and singer of the theme song *Swing, Little Girl* – woke up. The black dog was there, robbing him of his peace.

PART TWO

11

The Circus contains nothing that goes beyond his previous pictures. The movie is an infusion; unlovely things float to its surface. The Tramp has become bourgeois, his romantic existence a mere sham. In *The Gold Rush* he woos four women at the same time; here he contents himself with just one, and at the end, when he finally realises she doesn't love him, he generously gives her over to another man. He plays the selfless matchmaker, who sees others' happiness as more important than his own. On top of all the humiliation he suffers, he humbles himself as well, by playing the angel of happiness for others. This is him kneeling pathetically before those members of the audience who are reluctant to forgive him for his divorce from Lita, making a submissive plea: *take me up again! Can't you see: I want to be the way you want me to be!* He has betrayed the Tramp. He has used him for his own ends. He has betrayed art. The Tramp was his sole contribution to art. He didn't invent film, he didn't invent slapstick, the comedy chase, fighting with inanimate objects, the pie in the face, or the silent interplay of gesture and expression; Asta Nielsen was the best mime, Douglas Fairbanks the more versatile character actor. But he and he alone invented the character of the Tramp. He made it into an icon, which could proudly have taken a place alongside Don Quixote. *Could* have! – *if* the Tramp's final appearance had been in *The Gold Rush*. There could have been a glorious future in which his inventor would have got away with any escapade, any embarrassment, any flop, any drop in his artistic standards, because three words would have put the critics and mockers back in their place: *But the Tramp*! And in *The Circus* he has torn the mask of uniqueness from the Tramp's face; for the first time, he has made the world aware that he was wearing a mask. Underneath, you can see the philistine. *Don't you see? I'm just like you.* He has cut magical, anarchic scenes, like the Tramp acting as a "hand-shake facilitator" between a giant and a dwarf. The two of them are too far apart to give each other their hands. The audience wouldn't have got to see either the giant or the dwarf, just their hands, one from below, one from above. The Tramp provides the contact between them. – Out with it! – In *The Circus*, there are no big, bad, villains who bend gas lamps over to light their cigarettes, but who, at the same time, are doting fathers, and would set the whole world alight to prove it. Before, the Tramp was humiliated by objects, as if objects were gods. And people loved him for it. Where is the Tramp now? His charm has become a cowardly parody. *I'm just like you.* He has become a dull hysteric. The chase in the hall of mirrors is old vaudeville farce, made no more original by kicking policemen in the pants. The donkey is a relic from *The Gold Rush*, where it eats the Christmas decorations – here, it's just plagiarism, stretched out into a running joke which falls flat the second time around. Plagiarism comes from the Latin and means *selling one's soul*. There's nothing to add there.

This was what the howling and gnashing of the black dog sounded like.

First, he pulled the blankets over his head, just leaving a gap for his nose. That had always given him a gleeful sense of safety in the midst of an adventure: enemies were everywhere, but they couldn't see him, they would ride right over him. After a few minutes, he sat up in bed. There was nobody else in the house. He had even asked Kono Toraichi to leave – the butler, his right-hand man. Now he didn't want to be alone. This dog might be right, he told himself, but he was just barking in the dark, and he might only be right in the dark. He switched the light on. The black dog carried on howling and gnashing its teeth. It had already chewed its way through to his heart. Even so, Chaplin "felt certain" that the film contained no more than a few tiny errors which could easily be rectified.

At half past four in the morning he took a taxi to the studio. (Frank Kawa, the ever-cheerful chauffeur, and Harry Crocker, Chaplin's assistant, had also been told to take some time off.) He got out two blocks from the entrance. The driver knew who he was, of course: he asked if Chaplin wanted to stretch his legs for the last few yards, and grinned, which might have been a grin of solidarity – "great idea after a night on the tiles…" – or it might not have been. He wasn't going to the studio, he lied. And plodded off, unable to stop himself from putting a suggestion of the Tramp into his gait. The driver switched the engine off, but not the headlights. It might have been a kindly gesture. At that time of night the street lights were off, and the edge of the road was pitted with pot holes; it would have been easy to stumble. Or maybe it was gratitude, because the world's greatest comic was giving him a private performance in the dawn light. Or it might have been malice: you're being watched, Charlie. Don't forget what Lincoln said: you can fool all of the people some of the time, or some of the people all of the time, but not all of the people all of the time. Well, if he already thinks I'm a liar and a cheat, I'll give him the pleasure of being proved right, he thought; when he's munching his French toast at Hiram's, he can boast: I'm the one who really knows Charlie Chaplin. As he walked up the driveway to the studio building, he heard the car pull away.

The smell of the cutting room made him nauseous, and he only just managed to reach the restroom. He vomited in the wash basin. He coughed up green bile, his throat burned – he couldn't remember when he had last eaten anything. He rinsed out his mouth, gargled, pressed the side of his face against the cool wall tiles and closed his eyes.

There were full ashtrays on the little tables in the corridors. He had asked people repeatedly to empty the ashtrays at the end of the day, rather than the next morning, when cold smoke had seeped into the walls and ceilings, the curtains and carpets. It stank like a latrine. People were forbidden from smoking in his office. He had installed a compartment for chocolate under the writing surface of his desk, dark chocolate with candied hazelnuts or almonds. He tore open a bar, broke off a row of squares and chewed quickly. Then he fetched the seven reels of film from the safe.

He loaded the final reel and spooled through until just before the end.

12

The Tramp stands alone in the empty field. The circus wagons have left.

The Tramp sits down on a crate. Close-up. He looks sad.

There is a scrap of paper on the dirty ground in front of him. He picks it up. It has a star on it.

He looks at the star.

He screws up the paper.

He stands up, kicks the paper behind him with his foot and walks away. He walks away, in the centre of the frame. He is alone.

The End.

He cut out the shot of the Tramp looking at the star. Was he begging for grace from heaven? What else could looking at the star signify? The fact that he screws up the paper and throws it away didn't make the business any better, it just gave it a sour aspect. Does even he think himself unworthy of God's grace?

He went back through the action to the point where the Tramp is chased out of the circus.

The Tramp in his underpants. He stumbles. He's confused. Frightened. He's just performed a catastrophic high wire act. Everyone is shouting at him. He doesn't defend himself. He's given up. He has lost everything, his job, his love. Merna doesn't love him; she loves Rex, the tightrope walker. All is lost. He takes to his heels.

Intertitle: *That Night.*

The tramp is sitting by a fire. He has arrived back where he started. He has gained nothing. He is sad.

Merna turns up.

Intertitle: *"I've run away from the circus."*
She kneels before him.
"Can't you take me with you?"
He tries to persuade her. You're different, he tries to say, you're not one of life's losers like me. How can he give her hope? He thinks.
Intertitle: *"I've got an idea."*
He hurries back to the circus, and asks Rex to come to the woods with him and see Merna.
"I can do nothing for her."
He gives Rex the ring that he had intended to give her. He mimes rocking a baby in his arms, shows that soon a second and a third child will follow. The future of a happy couple. Rex considers this and makes up his mind:
"Take me to her!"
The Tramp leaps into his arms and kisses him, as if Rex were the man bringing him happiness, and not the man taking happiness from him.
Intertitle: *The Next Morning.*
Merna and Rex are getting married. The Tramp throws rice over the bridal pair. His face is a mask of panic and hysteria. It says: *I've given everything. Now forgive me!*

He cuts out the whole scene, six hundred feet of horrible self-abasement, six hundred feet of shame, six hundred feet of ass-kissing.
Now the empty field and the loneliness follow on from the scene where the Tramp is ejected in his underpants. The Tramp is thrown out of the circus. Cut. The circus leaves town. The Tramp sits alone. The Tramp leaves. The End.
But nobody was going to understand that ending. The cut had to be made earlier.
The Tramp is thrown out as a result of the high wire act he performs, in the belief that he will be held up by a strap around his waist. The strap comes off, as expected, and the Tramp has to walk

the tightrope without a harness. Then, a troop of monkeys starts getting in his way, biting his nose, pulling his trousers down. The audience shrieks in fright as the Tramp fights objects and animals – fights for his life. As he was lying awake at night, the film playing in his imagination, this was the only sequence he was completely satisfied with. He had spent six months learning to walk a tightrope for this performance. The crew had been bent double with laughter. He believed he'd opened up a new region of clown heaven, believed he could finally formulate the axiom of comedy: *the funniest a man can be is when he is staring death in the face. Only when we know death can we be funny. That's why animals don't laugh.* In the cold light of the early morning, the scene was good. But not good enough. It was without question the best scene in the film, but it wasn't as good as an average scene from his previous big pictures. That was the truth. And it was also the label that spelled destruction.

He cut out the whole section. Took the scissors to the reel further back, where the circus manager tells the Tramp he's giving him one last opportunity to make people laugh.

"I've had enough of this: you get one more chance."

The enraged manager pushes Merna to the ground; the Tramp wants to protest, he wants to stand up to the despot, but like a coward he runs away. He has missed his chance. The manager doesn't know that. The Tramp himself doesn't know it. Merna doesn't know it. Only the audience knows. – At least, the audience *should* know.

The circus leaves town. The Tramp sits alone. The Tramp leaves. The End.

That was dull. Or absurd. Or both. Not funny. Not clear. It might be right. But it had no poetry. But it was honest.

At around nine o'clock the first employees arrived: Olav Kaminski and Barry Goodell. These two were always first to arrive, because they came from the same bed and didn't want the others to know – though they were true enough to their orientation, themselves and each other not to make separate journeys from their shared home to the studio. They looked at him aghast, and crept away. Half an hour later, Sydney was standing in the cutting room. The film had already been cut by a third.

Sydney held his nerve. Nothing had been lost. Copies had already been made. The majority of the city's copying facilities had been booked out for *The Circus*, and they were working day and night.

"Do you need some pick-up shots?" he asked.

"No."

"What do you need?"

"A sound studio. Two sound technicians, no, make it three. And Merna, Harry, Allan, and if possible, Henry Bergman."

Sydney nodded and left.

By about midday, the film had been cut together at about half its original length. The sound studio had been booked, and the actors were waiting.

"Do you want to show me?" Sydney asked.

He watched the thirty-six minutes that remained of *The Circus* without saying a word.

Afterwards, he said: "The plot doesn't make sense any more. You'll have to write an awful lot of intertitles for people to be able to follow the story. Are we to have the intertitles spoken? Not write them and cut them in, but speak them? Is that why you wanted the studio?"

"No intertitles. Spoken or written. The intertitles have been liquidated. We'll recite poems over it. It's a lyrical film. A talking picture with images. An illustrated poem. It won't be a film, or a poem. It will be something new. Nobody is expecting this. Chaplin has exceeded all expectations, by fulfilling none of them."

"Who's going to recite the poems?"

"Merna, Harry, Allan, Henry...me."

"And what kind of poems?"

"I'll write them."

"When?"

"Today."

"How many poems?"

"I don't know, Syd. Free poems. Nothing to do with the circus."

"Then what will they be about?"

"Life. Poems about life, about death, about God, fate, joy, sadness, about everything except the circus. The circus is silent – it stands for life. Everything that exists is a metaphor. Nobody else is going to say I'm trying to capitalise on the success of Dupont's *Varieté* film."

"And the movie – or whatever we want to call it – won't be any longer than thirty-six minutes?"

"No...no...of course not...That's too short...Of course it will be longer than that."

"So you *are* going to shoot some pick-ups?"

"No. Some images can be stills. Like photographs...The world is moving, and then suddenly it stands still. Like Sleeping Beauty. That's new. That's poetry. Nobody's ever done that."

"That *is* new..."

"That's how we'll do it. We'll have single frames photographed. Get me a photographer – Leonard C. Wales, ideally. Esther can tell you where to get hold of him. And if he can't do it, ask Donald Saxon. And then we'll film the photographs. No experiments, I don't want any cameraman but Roland! And then I'll cut in the strips with the still images on them. Moving stills. That's the right thing to do. That's how we'll do it. And I'll compose all the music. It'll be wonderful – it's never been done before. It's not a movie, or pantomime, or a talkie, and it's not poetry. It's something new. The sound film has only just been born, and already it's been superseded. It's an art form that will bear my name. The audience will find a name for it. This is the birth of something entirely new, Syd! Can you feel it? You're the first witness. It's like...when Homer invented the epic."

"And how long do you want the film to be in the end, Charlie?"

"Sixty to seventy minutes. Like it was before. An evening's entertainment, as usual."

"So, twice as long as it is now."

"About that...yes..."

"So the audience is going to spend about half an hour looking at still images?"

At that, Chaplin broke down. Sydney closed the door to the cutting room, turned the key in the lock, put his arms around his brother and absorbed the convulsive sobs with his breast.

13

Sydney reminded him that the world couldn't hurt the Chaplin brothers; it had always been this way: people had always profited from them, not the other way round. Family came first, and art second, and their specific art form was really just a bit of fun that had started in the family to distract them from the hunger and the cold; he mustn't forget that. Everything that went beyond getting enough to eat, not freezing, a bed, not too soft and not too hard, was luxury – a marvellous thing, without a doubt, but not a necessity. He had worked out, he said, that the two of them would have laughed no less without luxury than they had with it.

"How do you work that out?" Charlie asked, taken aback.

"Inner statistics," said Syd in a bass voice. He dropped his lower jaw, his eyes staring and his mouth closed: he was imitating Buster Keaton, which was a running joke between him and his brother.

Charlie said what he always said in these situations: Syd would have been the better actor, and he was sorry to have taken that away from him. Syd replied as he always did in such situations: so what if that was true, it didn't matter, they'd still kept it in the family.

"The world doesn't matter all that much to us," he whispered in his little brother's ear, "not all that much, Carletto! Let's fleece it good and proper and stop worrying about it! It let us starve and freeze. It killed Dad and made Mum suffer. Now it has to pay. And if it doesn't cough up – *bene*. We'll kick it in the pants! People think a kick in the pants is a bit of fun. It isn't, we both know that! We can be different from the rest of the world. Do you think I'd hesitate to steal? If we needed to, I'd do it, you know that. And you'd do it too. You'd do it for me; I'd do it for you. We don't owe the world anything."

And so on...It helped.

It helped until after Christmas.

Charlie spent the holidays with Sydney and his wife Minnie in the San Gabriel Mountains. Syd advised him to travel without an entourage: he didn't need a secretary up there, or a butler, a chauffeur or a cook – life could go on without Kono Toraichi and Frank Kawa. Sydney hired a car and a driver and arranged a date for the return trip.

They took three rooms in a bed and breakfast. Simple, cosy, warm, light. Scents: baking, roasted meat, candles, floor polish. The only other guests were an older married couple. They both had white hair and smiled whenever they turned their faces to you, and they were discreet. Nobody showed any curiosity. Sydney had telephoned the proprietor and let her know that any curiosity would result in their immediate departure.

On Christmas Eve, they decorated the Christmas tree in the dining room. Charlie said his first words to Mrs Taylor, their hostess: she shouldn't go to any trouble on his account. At which she lowered her eyes and whispered that on the contrary, she was delighted to be able to go to some trouble on his account. Sydney raised his eyebrows, and she fell silent. That evening Charlie played a children's spinet. Dinner was a German roast with German side-dishes, calorific and delicious, with a crème caramel for dessert.

On Christmas Day, there was a tour of the Mount Wilson Observatory – an organisational master-stroke from Syd, as the station wasn't usually staffed over the holidays. A young scientist (he had passed up Christmas lunch with his wife and children for the privilege of shaking Charlie Chaplin's hand) gave a lecture, showed them the reflecting telescope, the largest in the world, explained how it worked, and said he was proud that Mount Wilson was the world centre for research into the galaxies. The weather was fitting, with clouds like swellings in a colicky sky. An ice-cold wind blew down from space and made patterns on the lake below the station.

Charlie was in high spirits that evening. Over dinner he told Minnie, Syd, the old couple and Mrs Taylor that in an instant, a film had come to him in its entirety: the Tramp on the moon, sprawling deserts beneath black skies, the man in the moon enters, characters from fairy tales and legends join him, even God makes an appearance, or maybe not, no, he does, the moon could be God's beach house on the sea of the universe...Sydney instructed Minnie to write down every word his brother uttered.

It was an enjoyable evening. Charlie acted out the Tramp's next adventure in space for the little audience in the snow-bound guesthouse, and Mrs Taylor said she had never laughed so much in her life – she couldn't even feel her sciatica.

Sydney was very relieved. The spark in his brother's eyes was a reassuring sign. He was in no doubt that Charlie had come through the crisis.

The day after Christmas, they drove back to Beverly Hills. Singing. First in three parts and then, after they had left the hairpin bends behind them, in four. The chauffeur, it turned out, was a more than passable tenor. He should drop by the studio in the next few days, Charlie said as they pulled into Summit Drive; only a good singer could sing in pantomime. Syd helped him carry the suitcases upstairs. Would he be alright alone in the house, he asked, was he sure, was he quite sure. Yes, of course, Charlie laughed.

But that night, the black dog returned. He didn't bark scorn and malice. He didn't bark at all. He sat in front of Charlie and stared him down.

14

The house was situated below Douglas Fairbanks and Mary Pickford's villa. They called their home "Pickfair". "You're invited to Pickfair, not to Doug and Mary's", as they always told their guests. With its forty rooms, the building was the most magnificent in the Hills. The park ran to fourteen acres; Doug liked to joke that some parts of it were still unknown to civilisation. By comparison, Chaplin's property looked modest. His house had fourteen bedrooms, three terraces and several balconies; from the lounge you could step out onto the marble slabs that surrounded the oval swimming pool, and a shady path led up to the tennis court through a little copse of fir trees. The house wasn't the largest, but it was the most beautiful in Beverly Hills – everyone said so. It was too big for him. It had been too big for him even when he was living there with Lita and the boys and Kono Toraichi and Frank Kawa and the rest of the staff. The house had always been full of people, coming and going, full of laughter, discussions, contests, tantrums, card games – and yet it was empty, false, hollow. It was hollow. It couldn't be filled. He had designed the house himself, with just as many rooms, only a third smaller than it was now. That had been at the start of the Twenties. A little later, Pola Negri had thrust herself into his life. "Sharlie, do you want our friends to say Chaplin's home is the gatehouse to Pickfair? I don't want that. Not I!"

The smallest room you could live in was the kitchen. It was functional, displaying hardly any signs of the architect's creative drive. Here he could cope with things, to some degree.

He lay awake, felt his heart stumble, and turned onto his right side, because he remembered a prophet saying you could extend your life if you didn't sleep on the side where your heart was. He could hear his own breathing. He tried to list the things he was afraid of, so he could dismiss the ones he was just imagining. He couldn't think of anything. He was frightened without being frightened. A single fear came to him: a prank he had played on Pola. They went to bed, put out the light, arranged the bedclothes around them, and he used the noise and the darkness to slip across to the end of the bed and sit silently on the mattress. Pola reached into his half of the bed and didn't find him there. "Sharlie?" she whispered. He said nothing. Gradually, she was able to make out the silhouette of the figure sitting on the end of the bed. "Sharlie, I know you're playing a joke on me." He didn't move. "Please, Sharlie, I'm frightened." He didn't move. "Sharlie, I'll scream, I'm really frightened." He was usually more afraid of himself than she was of him. They shrieked and turned the light on and embraced each other and laughed happily and rolled around. He thought he had been happiest with Pola. He hadn't loved her. And it took some effort to bring her features to mind, even though he'd studied them a thousand times on the cutting-room table.

He got up and groped his way out onto the staircase and down into the small lounge. He didn't dare switch a light on. Thinking about things repulsed him. He sat in the green velvet wingback chair by the fire and nodded off. Woke up freezing. He sensed a kind of futility rising like vapour from the armchair, misty, as if it had drifted into the house from far away.

He slept in small doses. And it was the same on the nights that followed. He switched from one room to another. He finally went back to the kitchen and lay down on the blankets and pillows in front of the range. He left the light on. The shiny, polished steel of the oven reflected his face. Its lower half showed signs of age. That's what he was: a young old man. This face didn't have the cut of a protagonist, but the ape-like expression of a stock character. The foolish face of a creature who feeds off applause. His hair had turned white. After the long break in filming, he had had to start dying it for continuity. He studied his reflection and couldn't find the Tramp.

Later he would try to explain to a reporter from a French newspaper that he had always suspected everything he did carried a deep meaning within it, but it had not been clear to him what this meaning was. The reporter would smile and nod and wouldn't understand; he wouldn't understand that Chaplin was talking about the Tramp, not himself. The same reporter would ask him if the Tramp's pale face didn't remind him of a skull. And Chaplin would answer, again, as if he was talking about someone else: "I've always been aware that the Tramp was playing with death. He plays with it, mocks it too, thumbs his nose at it, but every second of his life he's conscious of death, and that's why he is so frighteningly clear about the fact that he's alive."

He reached behind the bureau and pulled out the remains of the roll of paper that Buster Keaton had sent him the previous year; there wasn't as much left as he had hoped, though he still had enough to lie on. But then he left it there.

He would tell the same reporter: "The clown is so close to death that only a knife's edge separates them, and sometimes he crosses even this final line, but he keeps coming back. That's why he's not quite real – in a certain sense, he's a spirit." That night, he recalled, this certain sense had been turned inside out; it had become senseless.

On his third night alone at 1085 Summit Drive, the big house in Beverly Hills, he called Dr Van Riemsdyk. Asked him to come over and bring an "analgesic" with him. Complained of pains in his pelvis and leg.

"Severe pains?"

Yes, they were severe.

"In your pelvis and leg, you say?"

Yes, that was right.

"Which leg?"

He didn't reply.

After a long pause, Dr Van Riemsdyk said: "Mr Chaplin, I can't give you morphine. Are you listening? Did you hear me? And I know that's what you want. I can't. This is just nervous tension, and it will pass, believe me. I'll send you over a little bottle of a reliable household remedy, a mixture of valerian and passion flower."

He hung up. Without saying goodbye.

And then he called Raphael Brooks - the "bringer of consolation" as Mary Pickford called him.

An hour later Mr Brooks was at the door, waving up at him, a well-groomed man in a dark suit and a trench coat. He had brought everything with him. He advised Chaplin to undergo a three-day cure; the crisis would be over in twenty to forty hours. He just had to break the vicious circle of sleeplessness and senselessness. That was all. It was no big deal. The earlier the treatment was carried out, the faster the crisis would be over. He didn't know anyone who had become addicted because of a three-day cure. (Some people – and of course, he didn't say this – had stretched those three days out into three years, and Barbara La Marr never came back from her cure.)

The consolation consisted of eight ampules of heroin and a needle. Douglas had survived many crises in this manner. Mary, too, had found it beneficial. Neither of them had a bad word to say about Raphael Brooks. His name featured in all their friends' address books. He was unsentimental, they said, he didn't moralise, but he provided more precise information and had a better understanding of medicine than a dozen doctors put together. If Barbara had put herself in his hands, she would still be alive. At the time, heroin was all the rage in Hollywood: at every party there was a locked room, where it was laid out in thin lines on mirrors. The guest would ask the host with a wink: may I have the key to the refreshment room? Or: how do you get to paradise from here? The powder was snorted through rolled-up dollar bills. Raphael Brooks condemned this fad. Firstly, the stuff you got at parties was usually cut with something dreadful, and secondly, taking it in this manner damaged the lining of the nose. And only a very few people were aware of the correct dosage. He, on the other hand, guaranteed clean stuff and clean needles and information. True, the dose he recommended was a high one, but that made it more effective. A little heroin taken more often was many times more dangerous – that way, the body grew accustomed to it. This had two unfavourable outcomes: the depression didn't go away – in fact it got worse – and the patient became addicted. A short-term cure using a relatively high dosage blew away the depression without giving the body any chance to develop an addiction. Brooks likened depression to a burning oil well, and heroin to nitroglycerin.

Mr Brooks was a responsible man. With someone like Mr Chaplin, who was taking this cure for the first time, he insisted on a low-dose trial injection, the effect of which would not last long. Everyone's reaction was different. A small number of people couldn't tolerate heroin at all. They had to be helped in other ways. It was child's play, he said, to inject the heroin oneself, but still he saw it as his duty to stay with the patient on the first occasion. He would stay for two hours – that was included in the service.

Chaplin rolled up his shirt sleeve and allowed Mr Brooks to pull a rubber strap tight around his upper arm. He clenched his fist and stretched his fingers until the veins stood out in the crook of his arm. Mr Brooks rubbed a patch of skin there with alcohol and gave him the jab.

"You'll feel it in a second," he said, removing the strap.

A breath, and the heroin reached his brain. He felt as though his eyes were rolling back, and a warm wave rolled over his spine. He was sitting on a hard kitchen chair, with only his toes touching the ground, but he felt as though he were about to flow over the earth like melting wax. Before long he lost all self-awareness. He was at one with everything.

The effect lasted a little under an hour, then it grew flatter, and after another hour he landed.

"You should get some sleep now," said Raphael Brooks. "You'll sleep soundly. And when you wake up, you'll feel a lot better. But don't be tempted to stop the treatment because of that. On the contrary. If you feel good, that just means it's working. You'll be over the crisis in three days."

He nodded. He didn't want to talk. He could have, but he didn't want to.

Brooks handed him a neat, velvet-lined wooden box containing a fresh needle and seven ampules, and took his payment. The box was included, he said; Chaplin could keep it. It could be refilled at any time during future crises. He should have another injection before going to sleep, then one in the morning and one in the evening. If he had any problems injecting himself, he just had to call. Although further house-calls would incur a charge.

He lay down in front of the kitchen range, slept until late that night, and awoke with a feeling of total failure. From the filth of London to the filth of Hollywood – that's what they'd say about him. He was the most ordinary creature in the world and the uncanny spectre at the feast, united in one person. He no longer believed anything could help him, or that this was a crisis. He sat and stared. Then he drew the contents of all seven ampules into the syringe until the glass cylinder was full. He sat on the kitchen chair, his sleeve rolled up, the rubber strap around his arm. He pulled it tight, loosened it again, tightened it again, loosened it again. The point of the needle touched the greenish vein. Just like Raphael Brooks had showed him.

He slept and tried again. And slept and tried again.

At lunchtime on New Year's Eve he sent a telegram: "Charlie needs Winston."

The prompt reply: "Winston is coming."

15

Two days before the premiere, which was taking place in New York at Chaplin's request, *The Circus* was screened for a select audience. There were three dozen interested parties there: friends, critics, artists in other lines of work (among them the writers Sherwood Anderson and Dorothy Parker, and the painter William Glackens), scientists (including the later Nobel laureate Arthur Holly Compton), business people (not W.R. Hearst!), politicians (Joseph P. Tumulty, the former private secretary to President Woodrow Wilson, and Al Smith, Governor of New York and the Democrats' presidential candidate), and Douglas Fairbanks and Mary Pickford, of course, and Marion Davies, of course. The matinée was a tremendous success. The stand-out incident: Marti Hobson, a features writer for *Cosmopolitan* who had made it clear he was no friend to Chaplin, came up to him afterwards and – without taking the hand that was held out to him – said: "I would dearly love to slate your film, Mr Chaplin, and if it was good, I'd do it anyway, that's how unfair I am. But unfortunately it's very good, more than very good, and so I am compelled to praise it. And for that, I will never forgive you." The delicious thing about this, Chaplin remembered, was that Hobson's rage had been quite genuine. This *homme de lettres* left the lunch party, red-faced, to closet himself away and write a hymn of praise such as he would never write again. "That trickle-pisser" – to quote Sydney.

And with that, the black dog was driven away, or slunk off of his own accord – and with him went the memory of what he had been like. Yes, yes, said Chaplin in an interview, he would admit that in the last few weeks he had been "a little out of sorts, at times".

Sydney was already busy with preparations for the filming of

City Lights. He didn't want to see his brother unoccupied for a single day.

On January 5th, the day before the official premiere in the Strand Theatre, Churchill arrived in New York. He took a car straight to Chaplin's hotel and instructed the driver to wait outside the entrance. It was late afternoon, and there was still time for them to walk side by side through Central Park, as they had done a year before on Santa Monica Beach, and fight the black dog together. But the Mr Chaplin whom Churchill met was "hale and hearty, splendid-looking, in a truly buoyant mood".

Churchill described the following scene in a letter to Brendan Bracken. The detail-obsessed style of human observation here was typical of him – Charles de Gaulle once compared it, both admiringly and disparagingly, to Jean-Henri Fabre's method of studying insects.

He entered the lobby of the Waldorf Astoria, he wrote, "in civvies" (his way of saying incognito) and saw Chaplin standing at its centre, surrounded by photographers and various others: the curious, the important and the self-important. He was wearing a dinner jacket. Since their last meeting his hair had turned white at the temples, and there were a few white strands at the crown of his head as well. He was holding one of the bowls that usually stood filled with sweets on the lobby tables, and people were applauding as he balanced it on his forefinger like a circus plate-spinner. Then he held it upside down over his head with his right hand and placed the first two fingers of his left under his nose; everyone present instantly knew, without a doubt, that this was the Tramp – bowler hat and moustache. And then, as he jutted a hip into the off-kilter posture characteristic of the Tramp, which would make everyone think of the cane, without a doubt, his gaze travelled down the corridor of admirers and writers, and fell on Churchill. He hesitated for half a moment, then handed the bowl and the moustache

– the moustache too – to one of the ladies, windmilled his arms to create some space, and ran laughing towards him. But he had gone barely two steps before he seemed to realise *why* Churchill had crossed the Atlantic, probably striking precious time from his official diary and creating confusion among secretaries and ministers, and certainly being in a state of high anxiety about him, and he realised that it wasn't appropriate to be cheerful or funny, because these things demonstrated that the reason for the anxiety no longer existed. So he raised his arms abruptly and turned the joy into a lament, which was exaggerated and implausible, so he lowered his arms again immediately, probably intending to indicate someone at the mercy of his moods: on top of the world; in the depths of despair – technically speaking, manic-depressive. Was it feigned or real? Churchill looked at his friend, seeing how unpleasant, how embarrassing he was finding it to be in good health. He had forgotten to cancel the distress call! Churchill had gone to great trouble to support his friend in his hour of need, and the friend hadn't even gone to the small trouble of letting him know that he no longer required support. Charlie was ashamed: ashamed that he had abused their oath, and ashamed of his ill-advised pantomime.

"I knew," Churchill wrote, "that the truth was seldom to be seen in his face. But what does that mean? And: what truth? I could see *the truth of the clown*. It told me how things were with the person he was currently imitating. How I was, for example, when he imitated me. It didn't tell me how things were with him. He knew how to hide that truth. And if somebody succeeds in wringing that truth out of him, he will not have done a good thing."

The letter to Brendan Bracken ends: "But I am sorry beyond measure to have given this unique friend the feeling he had disappointed me. When a little lift of his eyebrow could do more for the health of my soul than could two handfuls of tablets."

Virginia Cowles, who had more time and opportunity to gain an insight into Churchill's heart than Charles de Gaulle did, said in one of her reflections that over the years, she had noticed that, for Churchill, close attention, microscopic observation and a detail-obsessed frenzy of description had been signs of an approaching bout of depression; as if he were mustering these faculties for a last look at the world, which would soon retreat and leave him in a dark, bleak place, sometimes for a long period. This remark occurred to me as I was reading Churchill's letter to Brendan Bracken. (A copy of the letter was among the documents that William Knott left to my father. Where the hand-written version is, I do not know. I would be interested to compare Churchill's handwriting at that time with his handwriting in other moods, to see whether the dog has left his pawprints there.)

In the days before and after the premiere of *The Circus*, Chaplin genuinely had very little time for Churchill. Marti Hobson's glowing review in *Cosmopolitan* heralded a change in public opinion. Alexander Woollcott of *The New Yorker* wrote: "...thanks to the witless clumsiness of the machinery of our civilization, someone [...] was actually permitted to have the law on Chaplin as though he were a mere person and not such a bearer of healing laughter as the world had never known". Manfred van der Laan, chief columnist of the *Chicago Tribune*, railed against the double standards which, he wrote, "nearly silenced one of America's greatest artists". Sydney pointed out van der Laan's imperialistic and unintentionally comic phrasing to Charlie, and in the hollow voice of the castle ghost, he scoffed: "Woe to America, when a British silent film star is silenced!" They laughed long and heartily, like they used to.

Chaplin, who for the past eighteen months had been first attacked and then shunned by the press, was handed from one interviewer to the next. He genuinely had very little time. But Churchill thought he was avoiding him.

It was three years before they saw each other again.

16

In February 1931 – three years after *The Circus* – *City Lights* was screened in London, at the Dominion Theatre. The city was overcome with a Chaplin hysteria that took everyone by surprise: the police, the hotel staff, Chaplin's entourage and, above all, Chaplin himself. He was swept away by it, quite literally: when the limousine was forced to stop two streets away from the hotel because of the crowd that had gathered outside, and Chaplin, who had no idea that he was the cause of all the excitement, got out to see what was going on, he was lifted by two gallant bodyguards and carried to the hotel, pushed along by the shrieking masses. Hundreds of hands reached out to him as people fought each other just to touch him, as if he were some kind of miracle worker. He found this enthusiasm bizarre, but he also enjoyed the fuss around him, particularly here in London, which he had once left as poor as a church mouse, on the shabby lower deck of the shabby SS Cairnrona – every child knew that story now. A crowd had gathered then, as well; the thirteen-year-old Princess Maria Viktoria, the darling of the British Empire, had just returned from Australia. But there had been fewer people on the quayside then than were now gathered outside the Carlton Hotel.

The British press – like the American press before them – hailed *City Lights* as *the* masterpiece of film art, a tragicomedy, as if – as Timothy Bedford said in the *Manchester Guardian* – "the spirits of Aeschylus and Aristophanes had come together". Had he been expecting such a reception, asked Carlyle Robinson, the press agent for United Artists. "Yes," Chaplin replied, plainly, defiantly, and untruthfully.

For a week, the Tramp occupied the front pages of all the

newspapers, his smiling face ousting the depressing announce-
ments about the global economic crisis.

Lady Astor invited him to lunch at Cliveden, the grand seat of the
British branch of her family. Her invitations were legendary; the
press reported on them as if every visit was a state visit and she was
the foreign minister. She represented the Tories in the House of
Commons, but her views were liberal and her lifestyle eccentric, and
this was reflected in her choice of guests. She was friends with the
economist John Maynard Keynes, who was seen as revolutionary,
the radical dramatist George Bernard Shaw, and the no less radical
H.G. Wells, who sympathised with Soviet Russia and campaigned
for the abolition of the monarchy. Also present were David Lloyd
George, Ramsay MacDonald and Stanley Baldwin – the first was a
former Liberal prime minister (and at that point, the only Liberal
prime minister); the second, a member of the Labour Party and
current prime minister; the third, the former Conservative prime
minister and MacDonald's predecessor. The man who went on to
lead the British fascists, Oswald Mosley, was also invited. As was
Winston Churchill.

Lady Astor didn't know that Churchill and Chaplin were friends.
She meant to use Chaplin to show off to everyone, and Churchill
to show off to Chaplin. She didn't place the three prime ministers,
the two writers or the economist on a par with these two; only
Winston, she said on another occasion, shone as bright as Chaplin.

Churchill did not shine. He stood apart from the others, spoke
little, and drank nothing (as everyone noticed). He looked ill,
puffy, purplish. Chaplin sought him out and they shook hands
and exchanged a few words, though none about their last meeting
in New York. Churchill declared he was "rather taken with" *City
Lights*, a faint phrase that still disconcerted Chaplin even years
later. The scene with the stone at one end of the rope and the neck
at the other, said Chaplin, did he remember, they had come up with

it together in the wilderness of the Malibu Hills. "No, no," Churchill muttered, "Mr Chaplin came up with it; I just had the honour of watching him do it."

Lady Astor asked Churchill to propose a toast. He obeyed, speaking in a soft voice, searching for words, his back hunched as if he was in pain: "My lords, ladies and gentlemen," he began, and went on to say that there had once been a lad from the other side of the Thames who had gone out into the world and won everyone's heart. He indicated Chaplin, sitting opposite him. He tried to say his name, but his voice failed him, and the guests had to read it from his lips. It wasn't intentional. But that's how it was understood – he didn't need to say who he meant.

Chaplin was in a state of high excitement, which led him to commit a faux pas. He stood up and began in the same way, with "My lords, ladies and gentlemen", before addressing a few words to everyone, and a few to Churchill, calling him "my friend the late Chancellor of the Exchequer". And in case anyone there had missed this embarrassing error, his embarrassment compelled him to add: "Well, it seems peculiar to say the 'ex-Chancellor of the Exchequer'".

Lloyd George, Baldwin and MacDonald must have been secretly delighted at Chaplin's clumsy words – the first because Churchill had switched to join his Liberal Party to get one over on the Conservatives, and, on the party's left wing, had given it more trouble than service as Home Secretary; under the second, once Churchill had switched sides again, he had risen to become Chancellor of the Exchequer, though he stepped down from the shadow cabinet after the Conservatives lost the election, to the party's great relief; and the third, the incumbent Labour prime minister saw Churchill as a devourer of socialists and oppressor of workers, and party enemy number one.

Churchill invited Chaplin to Chartwell – made a point of inviting only him! At his country seat he showed him the swimming pool, which he had excavated and walled in himself, and the duck pond and the guest house, which were both still half-finished. But he was rather distant, behaving as if Chaplin were a stranger, quickly excusing himself and leaving his wife, Clementine, to look after their guest.

17

Chaplin stayed in London for two weeks, giving parties, being invited to parties, acting first the playboy and then Till Eulenspiegel, involving himself in romantic entanglements, giving countless interviews, and making a game out of telling the *Observer* the exact opposite of what he had announced to the *Evening Standard* a few hours previously. The rumour went around that Ramsay MacDonald had suggested knighting him, as did the rumour that Queen Mary had vetoed it. At one point Chaplin said it would be the greatest honour for him to be received by the queen, and soon afterwards he started telling witty anecdotes about having recently been offered the role of a knight, but finding the screenplay too bad. Some of the press were amused, others were indignant; they knew very well how to interpret stories of this kind, and Chaplin was practically insulting the monarchy. He apologised, and the next day made fun of himself for having apologised. He enjoyed playing Puck.

And then suddenly, he stopped enjoying himself. In London, at least.

He set off without warning, leaving half of his entourage behind. He crossed the Channel and took the train to Berlin, in a private carriage placed at his disposal gratis by Lady Astor. He met Marlene Dietrich there for dinner at the Hotel Adlon. Prince Heinrich of Prussia showed him round the ostentatious buildings of Potsdam; he visited Albert Einstein and was impressed by his modesty, witnessed a Nazi rally, and heard a speech by one Dr Goebbels. He couldn't believe this man was a politician and not a colleague of his – nobody could listen to him without laughing himself sick, he said. Did he speak English, this great clown? A man like that could easily start a career in sound films and earn a lot of money. Shame Sydney wasn't there: he would have done the deal. Peter Lorre and Celia Lovsky, who had accompanied Chaplin, dragged him away, afraid that someone might recognise him – although his hair had turned white and off-screen he now looked hardly anything like the Tramp. If Chaplin had been able to speak German, they said, it would have taken him no more than a few words to realise that this man was anything but funny, and was certainly no clown. The Nazi propaganda paper *Der Stürmer* had printed a hate-filled article about Chaplin, the "sensuously insatiable American fidgeting Jew".

His journey took him onward to Vienna; a crowd of thousands awaited him there as well. It was only with the help of the police, who formed a cordon around him, that he managed to get through to the Hotel Imperial. He would have liked to visit Sigmund Freud, but unfortunately Sigmund Freud could not be visited.

His next destination was Venice: gondola ride, Doge's palace, Rialto Bridge, dinner with the writer Massimo Bontempelli, who treated him to a lecture on Mussolini and the glorious future of fascism. And finally, Paris! There were letters from Sydney waiting for him at the hotel. His brother didn't press him to cut short his travels, he merely enclosed a collection of all the ideas Charlie had noted down or dictated over the past few years for a new film, a film full of social criticism and class warfare. Sydney knew that ultimately there was only *one* temptation his brother couldn't resist: work.

But Charlie did manage to resist. In mid-April, on his brother's birthday, he met Sydney in Nice and convinced him to let his duties rest for a little while. They travelled to North Africa together, which was funny and fascinating, and came back to France via Spain, having received a death notice: Ralph Barton had taken his own life in New York.

Ralph Barton had been a well-known caricaturist and, until the previous year, a sought-after illustrator. He had always been regarded as a difficult man, but he had finally proved too difficult for his employers and they had stopped using him. It seemed as if this man was incapable of agreeing to anything, which made every bit of business with him into a long, drawn-out affair. But Chaplin had been fascinated by him; he didn't know any artist but Ralph whom you could watch creating his art. "Put something in his hand, a stylus or a stone or a piece of chalk or charcoal, and say: lion! Or: T.S. Eliot! Or: the angel Gabriel! And he'll draw whatever you want on paper or asphalt or a board or a napkin. He gets straight to work, doesn't hesitate for a second, and doesn't break off the line until he's finished. His hand is guided by a higher power." This quotation had been printed on the back cover of a book of selected drawings by Ralph Barton. The two of them had been friends ever since. When Chaplin was told that Ralph had made a suicide attempt after a woman had left him, he invited him on the spur of the moment to accompany him to England and across Europe. They had great fun in London, less in Berlin, and none in Vienna. Barton really was a difficult man. His moods became tyrannical, and his paranoia could be truly vexing. Everyone was glad when he finally left the little group in Venice. Even Chaplin. Nobody took his constant threats of suicide seriously; they thought these were pure blackmail, and nothing more. And then he really did take his own life.

The French film director Abel Gance, who accompanied Chaplin on his travels for a little while, told him that Churchill was currently staying in Biarritz; the unemployed boss-man was finally minded to take a holiday, which, as everyone knew, he'd had no opportunity to do in the last twenty years.

"He said that?"

"That is apparently what he said, yes."

"Did you speak to him?"

No, Gance had not. His information came from the poet and actor Antonin Artaud, who had interviewed Churchill for a surrealist magazine and had, he said, been absolutely charmed by him, by his wit and his repartee; his answers had been entirely monosyllabic.

"And how did he seem otherwise? Serious? Cheerful? Absent-minded? Angry? Sad?"

Gance didn't know.

Chaplin wanted to visit his friend in Biarritz, alone. He was still feeling guilty about his faux pas during the lunch with Lady Astor (particularly as someone had told him that "the Late Chancellor of the Exchequer" had become Churchill's nickname in the House of Commons), and he was still feeling guilty about neglecting him three years earlier in New York, when he was celebrating the premiere of *The Circus*. He blamed himself for the fact that relations between them had cooled. Ralph Barton's suicide had shaken him to the core; he hadn't wanted to see anyone for a whole day. But his thoughts were not of poor Ralph, he had to admit that to himself, and he felt guilty about that, too – they were of his lonely friend on the Atlantic coast. He had never – alas! – been seriously concerned about Ralph, but he was about Winston. He had never made a pact with Ralph, but he had with Winston.

He met a "man without a mood".

18

At the Hotel du Palais they told him Churchill was down on the beach. He was painting.

That was how Chaplin found him: wrapped in a stained coat and wearing a straw hat fastened under his chin with a leather lace, sturdy shoes, and woollen gloves with the fingers cut off. He was sitting on a folding chair and had worked the legs of his easel into the sand; in his right hand he held the paint palette and in his left the brush; there was a cigar clamped between his teeth. He was painting the white lighthouse on Cape Hainsart and the cliffs below it and the beach and the sea with its white-capped waves. No birds. No people.

It was early September, and the wind from the Atlantic brought salty air with it and drove knots of cloud in front of the sun, changing the light suddenly from bright to dull and dismal. But in the picture on the easel, Chaplin recalled, an eternally blue summer sky stretched out over land and sea. The picture – this was his first impression – told a different story to his friend's expression. His face was half hidden by the scarf he was wearing under the hat, a fragment of a face; it spoke of sorrow and anger, more anger than sorrow. If the camera had shown his face first, everyone in the theatre would have believed the painter was working on some kind of lampoon, a caricature, each stroke of his brush made with disappointment and contempt, with the intent to avenge and insult. But the picture showed a peace that didn't exist in reality, and could only be interpreted as a symbolic reflection of inner happiness. How wrong that interpretation would have been! And how wrong was the interpretation of the expression on the artist's face!

He laid a hand on his friend's shoulder, Chaplin said, gently, so as not to alarm him, and in a soft voice, but articulating the words clearly – something he had felt was missing from the sound films he'd seen – he said:

"It's me, Charlie."

He meant to bridge the distance between them from the very start – something he'd failed to do in New York and at Lady Astor's house.

"It's me, Charlie," he said again straight away – this time a little more theatrically. On the one hand, if you took the pathos seriously, it was intended to suggest: *I came to help you*; or on the other hand, if you took it as being ironic, it could have meant something like: *you're Don Quixote; I'm Sancho Panza. Together we'll be defeat the windmills* – something like that.

Churchill laid down another two, three, four brushstrokes and then turned to him.

"Oh," he said, and carried on painting.

I am quoting from Josef Melzer's book where he, in turn, gives a three-page-long quote from Chaplin:

"I know –" (Melzer mentions that Chaplin kept interrupting his story and his thoughts and falling silent for long periods, though whenever Melzer tried to ask a question, he would fend him off with a wave of his hand)

–I know that most people on earth will regard it as unseemly or even malign: exploiting a friend's suffering for one's own artistic ambitions, observing it meticulously in order to be able to reproduce it later. From a mean-spirited viewpoint, artists are indeed unseemly and malign. The black dog was visiting my friend. And he had him by the throat. Choking off his words. This French writer and actor who interviewed him for his magazine must have been blind if he thought Winston was giving him witty repartee – or maybe he only saw what he wanted to see. He really was monosyllabic. The second syllable, and the third and the fourth, were snatched away and devoured by the dog. I'd come at the right time. Later he told me that was the worst bout of depression he'd ever had, and the longest – and, at least until its *peripeteia,* he had only been able to get through the day because he knew his Browning was waiting for him in his suitcase, under his shirts. I asked him why he hadn't called on me, as we'd agreed. He said he didn't have the strength for it. I believe he didn't trust me any more. And he had every reason not to. I had let him down in New York, and at Lady Astor's. And I'd let him down this time as well. I'd come even though he hadn't called me. And that, too, would count against me. Now I was here. I was with him. But I was no better than this actor and writer with his interview. I wasn't blind, but I too saw only what I wanted to see. This ineffable picture! An old man, older than he really is, a great deal older, sitting on the beach slumped in his chair, holding onto his hat and his easel by turns to stop the storm blowing them away, struggling against the dog at his throat and in his soul by conjuring an idyll onto his canvas. A man without a mood, filled to bursting with nothing, a life spent playing catch-up. In the hour we spent on the beach, all I could think was: this could be a scene in a film. And for the first time in my life I thought: it could be a scene in a sound film. Not just a scene, it could be a whole film! And not a studio production! I'd shoot it in Biarritz, on that exact spot, not one foot to the right, not one foot to the left. Winston had fixed on the only correct spot. Two men meet on the beach, and everything you see is different from how it really is. Such a thing had never been represented in an artwork before. At least not with the potency of what I could see in my mind's eye. Only film can do that. No, I thought – and I was surprised at myself – I thought: *only sound film can do that!* I could have danced down the beach! At that moment, I had invented the sound film! What were the pictures that had been shown in cinemas before – *The Jazz Singer,* or *Lights of New York,* which I had liked more – they were nothing but theatre on film! Documentary films. Documenting theatre. But what I could see before me, as a finished artwork, was a *true* sound film, a talking picture. *The first talking picture*! You couldn't convey the words that were spoken there in pantomime. The philosopher says: he who speaks incurs debts. I had tattooed this maxim on the inside of my forehead. But the only way to pay off your debts is to go on speaking. He who speaks must go on speaking. Chaplin's first talkie! And it goes without saying that only actors in our club would be capable of acting in this, the first real sound film. A two-hander. Title: *Two Gentlemen on the Beach*. Cast: *Buster Keaton and Charlie Chaplin*. Who else? I mean, really, who else! Nobody would have seen that coming. Chaplin as anti-Chaplin. Life, as it is! Life doesn't consist of three acts or five acts, it's not a drama. Life is a revue: one scene after another, with no order to them. Speech as *sprechgesang*. The eternal recurrence of the same. Every word a signature tune. Light is day, and darkness night. No metaphors! Film has always been interested in the remarkable. A good film transforms a thing that is merely remarkable into an enigma. It does that by showing *what is*. Where might an excess of reality lead? The logical answer would be: a film in colour. In Milton, Adam has hyacinth-coloured curls, and so does Homer's Odysseus... I sat down on the sand beside Winston. But instead of fighting the black dog alongside him, which was my duty as a friend, I was sitting in my own private cinema, looking up at a screen as big as the inside of my forehead, watching and wondering and listening and saying nothing. Winston would have understood. I told him about it later, and he understood. I said to him: 'Ever since humans have been able to speak, everything we see is different to how it really is.' This realisation, I told him, had come to me that afternoon on the beach in Biarritz. And it's true. That was why I wanted to remember the scene as accurately as possible. And that was why that night, in my hotel room, I took minutes from my memory. It was why I was so attentive. It was why I was so inattentive.

Chaplin left the following morning with the bitter feeling in his breast that he had let his friend down yet again. He quickly got himself another abominable headline in the *Daily Herald*, which said he had bent a fork into the shape of a pistol and taken aim at a reporter who had asked him when the world would get to see the Mafia play that he and Churchill had concocted in this rarefied atmosphere.

He travelled to England, did this and that and nothing. In November he sent a telegram to Churchill from Dover:

Apples, peaches, pears and plums
Tell me when your birthday comes.

He did this and that and nothing.

He was intending – as I mentioned – to stay in London over Christmas and visit the orphans at the Hanwell Schools; but when he heard about Churchill's accident in Manhattan, he set off for New York at once – this time, he wanted to do it right – got past the butler and the nurse who refused to believe that he was Charlie Chaplin, and found Churchill – in the "best possible mood", sitting up in bed, surrounded by books and manuscripts.

"And the easel? The paints? The brushes?" he asked breathlessly.

"They're not mine," Churchill replied, knowing what his friend meant. "You don't need to worry, Charlie. This is my cousin's house. She's a painter. She's allowing me to stay in her studio while I recover from my duel with a Chrysler DeSoto."

For a week, Chaplin visited his friend every day, staying for several hours each time. Churchill painted a portrait of him. The left-handed man painted with his right hand, as his left had been injured in the accident. Chaplin said he thought true art was made in this way, namely from a lack, and judged the result to be "terribly beautiful". Churchill wrote to his wife that he had never laughed so heartily in all his life. If Mr Chaplin should ever find himself in trouble, "I will stage a coup if necessary and lead the Royal Navy in to get him out." Joy was a raw material that the British Empire depended upon as much as coal, rubber and tea.

19

Chaplin's Virtue. That was the title Chaplin wanted, Josef Melzer writes. As naive as it might sound, as he approached death he was keen to gather "arguments for God's grace".

At one point during the interview, in the middle of another subject entirely, he asked: "Do you believe, Monsieur Melzer...and please tell me the truth now...do you believe...that God in heaven has watched any of my films?"

Melzer relates this story in an afterword to the second edition of his book. We shouldn't forget, he says, justifying the delay, that the first edition was published just after Chaplin's death, and Chaplin's reputation as an artist had suffered hugely after his last films. A lot of critics denied that silent film had any real artistic merit, seeing it merely as a kind of prehistory, in the same way *Commedia dell'arte* had been a kind of prehistory to Shakespeare's plays. A few said that, when viewed at a distance, it was clear that Buster Keaton, W.C. Fields, Harold Lloyd, Stan Laurel and Oliver Hardy or, later, the Marx Brothers, were not only on a par with Chaplin, who had been idolised for far too long, but even ranked above him. And unlike him, they had secured themselves and their genre from the sound film with great dignity – and without embarrassments like *A Countess from Hong Kong* – or had made the move into sound with confidence.

Melzer was cut to the quick, he says, by Billy Wilder's review of Chaplin's autobiography, and by the memory of how Chaplin reacted when they talked about it: he seemed hurt by it in a way Melzer had not thought possible – after all, it had happened four years previously. It was a hatchet job, not a critique, and it was aimed at Charlie Chaplin himself, not at the book; you could sense a degree of contempt and hatred behind it against which fame, works, and even arrogance were no defence. Most of all, Chaplin was hurt to find that Wilder had sniffed out his own fears with the instinct of an inquisitor. It was as if Wilder had stepped straight out of his nightmares and tattooed the black dog's bark onto his forehead with a red-hot needle:

"Chaplin was a giant, as long as he played his silent little tramp. As soon as he opened his mouth, painful banalities came out...He was like a child of eight writing lyrics for Beethoven's Ninth...With all the erudition of a Reader's Digest subscriber, he threw big words around: socialism, citizens of the world, universal brotherhood... It's enough to make you weep: a thoroughgoing genius leaves his familiar territory and makes a fool of himself – as if Michelangelo had climbed down from the ceiling of the Sistine Chapel to put on ice-skates and dance with Sonja Henie."

"It was not a time," Melzer writes, "when naivety was a valued quality in an artist." He didn't want to compromise Chaplin, and so he'd left the story that follows out of the first edition of his book – although it is where the title, *Chaplin's Virtue*, comes from. He feared his protagonist's thoughts might come across as ridiculous, and be made more ridiculous by being merely set down in words – without looking into Chaplin's eyes as he spoke, without following his gestures, sensing his enthusiasm, experiencing the physicality that still spoke volumes even in his old age.

Now (this was ten years later), people had stopped trying to diminish Chaplin's genius, and only the ever-dull cynics would mock his naivety.

When Chaplin spoke about the feelings that governed him during his work, his words had all the fervour of a mystic who has experienced a divine revelation.

Once he said: "Picasso didn't believe in Him, but he was still sure there was at least one of his paintings hanging in heaven...I'm sure He won't have seen all my films, that would be too much to ask...

It would be enough for me if He'd watched *The Kid*...no, *The Gold Rush*, what do you think? What would you advise him, Monsieur Melzer? Einstein would tell Him to watch *City Lights* – that much I know. If it was *Limelight*, I'd want to re-cut a few scenes first, take out a few altogether, if possible..."

The whole interview stretched over five long working days, Melzer writes; and Chaplin was never as serious as he was in this particular half-hour. As if it were the last thing he wanted to say in his life – half speaking to this world, and half to the next.

He returned once more to the episode in the Biltmore Hotel in Los Angeles in February 1927, when he and Churchill had formed their alliance against the black dog and the thirteen-year-old Sarah had come to join them because she couldn't sleep. Churchill had meant to compliment him in front of his daughter when he said Chaplin could imitate anyone in the world. At Sarah's request, he had played her father, and played him so well that she was torn between delight and horror, and cried out, "More! More!" – loudly at first, laughing, then becoming ever more quiet and serious, until finally she put her hands over her eyes and started shaking her head.

"Shall we ask Mr Chaplin if he can do someone else for us?" Churchill asked his daughter.

"Who?" she said.

"You think of someone! Someone you and Mr Chaplin both know."

"I don't know anyone, Pomp."

"Would you like him to do the American president?"

"I don't know him."

"The king?"

That didn't particularly interest her.

"Ebenezer Scrooge?"

That was silly, he didn't exist, he was made up.

"Should he play the Tramp?"

"But he *is* the Tramp, Pomp."

"No, Sarah, he's Mr Charles Chaplin."

"I really can't think of anyone."

"Well, I can think of someone!" Churchill cried out. "Shall we ask him if he can play you, Sarah?"

That made them all laugh – Sarah, her father, and Chaplin – and Sarah said: "He can't do that, Pomp, he's much too old."

"He could play you as you'll be twenty-five years from now," her father said.

She didn't want that.

And then, said Chaplin fifty years later, Sarah made a remarkable suggestion.

He should play himself, she said.

It reminded him of Eva Lester and her theory that an artist deceived God with his art. He thought to himself: I am myself, as God made me, but the Tramp is me as *I* have made me, and the Tramp is better, and that is my deception. Lita's lawyers may be scoundrels, but only because they're exaggerating; at bottom, they're right. I am what they say I am: vain, selfish, avaricious, domineering, brutal, reckless, spiteful, lecherous. But I created someone who is better than me. And therein lies my virtue.

"I can't," he said. "I can't play myself. And in any case it's quite enough that I am who I am. The fewer people see me at it, the better."

Churchill was amused. But Sarah gave him another look, which made him believe that in his face she could read the thoughts he hadn't put into words; that she could see him as he really was, without him playing himself; and that she had already had thoughts similar to his own.

To Josef Melzer, he said: "A life full of vice, and only a single virtue." That was why he wanted Melzer to call his book *Chaplin's Virtue*.

"I'm not an idiot, as Mr Wilder believes me to be, and I'm not naive, I'm not even happy. Only a happy idiot can maintain his naivety over a whole lifetime. Everyone else lays it aside eventually, or loses it. Most people grow stubborn and angry about it. Better never to have been naive. My brother Syd and I never had the opportunity to be. Happily. Or unhappily."

This quote ends Melzer's afterword to the second edition of his book.

PART THREE

20

Clementine Churchill's concern was for her husband; she was "resigned to living with it", as I read in the pages from her diary that have been preserved. It was a concern that often "took an almost detective-like attention", though it didn't make her "feel guilty". She had always been aware, she said, that Winston was "driven", and that any attempt at actively looking after him would therefore have no effect; it would merely be found tiresome. She saw her task as "sweeping the path, putting up warning signs, padding the sharp corners", and above all, "preparing myself and the family for catastrophe". She looked into her husband's heart, and although she saw the lust for life that was as much admired as it was vilified, and meant every newspaper profile described him as a "Renaissance man", she saw an aversion to life lurking alongside it, and she knew it was no less powerful than its sparkling counterpart. And in any case: who could promise that this "drive" would exert a stronger force over her husband than his destructive powers? "He doesn't fear death," she wrote. "Sometimes he desires it. He would swallow it like a tablet." The thought that he might take his own life had been with her ever since they were married. She was prepared at all times to receive the news.

Her concern for her son, however, did make her feel guilty. He clearly drank too much. He had started drinking at the age of fifteen. His parents hadn't exactly been guiding stars. After Stan Carrick, Winston's chauffeur, had pulled Randolph out of the gutter one night a hundred yards from their London flat, dragged him home and took a beating for his pains, Clementine had started to avoid drinking alcohol in Randolph's company. She fell silent when he appeared; she looked to one side or up or down and arranged things so she would never be alone in a room with him. Winston didn't see any harm in his son's "excess"; on the contrary, he would clear his diary for a night of excess with him – Champagne, brandy, whisky, tobacco.

A friend warned him that he had spoiled Randolph rotten as a child, and now those pigeons would come home to roost. Winston didn't share his opinion. "Young people," he liked to say, "do what they want. The only time a parent really has control over their children is before they are born. After that, their nature develops inexorably, one step at a time." He encouraged – or, as the same friend put it, forced – Randolph to be his comrade, his confidant, his sidekick; when he went to meet the great and the good, he brought Randolph along. And he *didn't* tell him to keep his mouth shut. Randolph was to speak up whenever he thought he had something to contribute to the conversation. And so he did, in a loud, clear voice – which sounded a little too tyrannical to some people's ears.

Diana, two years older than her brother, was the "settling-in child". When I read this expression and saw what it meant, a shudder ran through me, and I skipped to the end of her story: "Puppy Kitten", as she called herself in her childhood, took her own life at the age of fifty-four, having worked for the Samaritans and devoted a great deal of time to people contemplating suicide. But then her back-ache returned, and one night it became unbearable. What her father called the "black dog", she called her "backache". "Puppy Kitten hurts here, and here, and all the way up here!" she had cried as a child when she wanted someone to rub her back, and when she was sad her father would ask: "Does Puppy Kitten have backache?", and he would rub her back. When she departed this world, the sun still had to rotate twice more around the earth before he followed her. From that day on, he kept his eyes on the ground, and mur-mured to himself over and over: "Not any more. Not any more."

When asked what he meant by this, he replied: "I'm too old to do that now. It's too late. It's too late even for that. One should not put it off so long."

The settling-in child received little attention. Diana wasn't difficult like Randolph, or artistic and ambitious like Sarah, her father's favourite. She was a long way from being as pretty as Sarah, whose titian-red hair made her stand out in any company. She wasn't as clever as Mary, the youngest, nor did she have her essentially likeable personality. She drank. But unlike Sarah and Randolph, she was ashamed of it and suffered for it. She was the first in the family to use the word "addiction" in connection with alcohol. She didn't make jokes about it like her father did – "I'm not an alcoholic: no alcoholic could drink as much as I do". She didn't speak in public, and avoided interviews, no matter what the subject. She doesn't seem to have had many friends. She liked being alone – and was afraid of it at the same time. When she was alone, she drank. She would sometimes have an "attack of nerves". These were sudden breakdowns, with no prior warning, which couldn't be interpreted as the symptoms of any illness. She is seldom mentioned in biographies of her father, and she is the only one of Churchill's children who doesn't appear in his autobiographical account of the Second World War.

William Knott, by contrast, wrote about her frequently in his letters to my father. The two of them didn't meet very often – during the war, Diana was with the Women's Royal Naval Service, and Knott was at her father's side, wherever he happened to be – but a few encounters sufficed to establish a mutual sympathy. Like Mary, whom Knott only came to know later, there was nothing haughty about Diana, but unlike her she was serious and overly cautious. Still, she wasn't a closed book, or at least she hadn't appeared so to Knott; on the contrary, she spoke candidly to him about her parents and siblings. Diana was also the only Churchill who stayed in touch when his service came to an end. Mary only made contact with him again two years after her father's death.

Clementine didn't worry about her daughter Diana. In another context, she once said – and Churchill's biographer Virginia Cowles remembers the exact wording – "One doesn't worry about those one loves most, but about those who pose the greatest threat to one's own wellbeing." Worry was nothing more than "selfishness in disguise". Diana obviously posed no such threat.

21

At the time of the incident I am preparing to recount, which forms the first high point in my story – Munich, April 1932 – Diana was engaged to John Milner Bailey, the son of Sir Abe Bailey, a rich South African friend of her father's. The wedding was to take place in December. Diana was twenty-three, and John thirty-two. It wasn't that the two of them had had no choice in the matter – there had been no agreements made behind their backs; they had been spoken to quite openly, individually as well as together – the families had merely "suggested" the match. Diana and John hardly knew each other; she had not impressed him, nor he her. They said as much in the first words they exchanged in front of their parents, having taken a walk together in the park at Chartwell at the latter's request. On their return, they both described the atmosphere between them as neutral. Winston argued that this was the ideal basis for a fruitful marriage: if a husband and wife had a long, intense relationship, and were passionately in love before their marriage, then the cooling-off period would begin with the wedding. All their lives, the marriage would have a stale aspect, a sense of dissatisfaction provoked by the memory of the time before. But for them, love and passion would flourish in the same ground at the same time.

As Winston had prophesied, shortly after their engagement the pair – independently of each other – said that they did not now consider falling in love over the coming months an unrealistic possibility.

To encourage these feelings, Winston suggested that they take a final family holiday together – some time to enjoy each other's company, a trip through the Netherlands, part of France, and most importantly Germany – the Rhineland, Hesse, Bavaria. They didn't have to stick together at all times – a few days as a family, then one of them might go elsewhere, friends would join them, then he and Clementine and little Mary would be alone again, then they would all gather round the table together – just as each of them wished, all circling around each other: a vacation, in short. A vacation, as if they had nothing to do.

At that time, Winston really did have nothing to do – apart from his work as an MP in the Lower House, where he was one of the most prolific speech-makers; and apart from writing regular columns for *The Strand Magazine*, the *Sunday Pictorial*, the *Daily Mail*, *The Times*, the *Saturday Review*, *Answer*, *The Sunday Telegraph*, *Sunday Chronical*, *Sunday Dispatch*, *The Sunday Times*, the *Evening Standard*, the *News of the World*, the *Jewish Chronicle,* the *Daily Telegraph* and a series of other English and American newspapers and magazines, sometimes two, sometimes three or four articles per week (an MP's salary could be described as symbolic, and not even just measured against the Churchills' lifestyle. Winston had lost a significant part of his fortune in the Wall Street Crash, but wasn't willing to make even the slightest cutback in his and his family's lifestyle, so he had come to rely on his income as a columnist – a "paid hack", as he said self-deprecatingly, though he also said it with pride, probably knowing that his articles earned him more than double the prime minister's salary); and apart from completing an apprenticeship as a bricklayer and, together with his master Harry Whitbread, building a sixty-five-foot-long wall, a guest annex, a swimming pool and a pond, raising ides and two black swans in the last of these, and planting a rose garden around it, not inferior in terms of exclusivity to His Majesty's rose garden; and apart from "Marycot", the brick playhouse with a fireplace and a miniature kitchen range that he had built for his youngest daughter Mary without any help. Apart from all that, he really did have nothing to do. He was on the outside. The power was inside.

He had bidden it farewell.

One morning – "in the best possible mood, a glance at the sun, a mighty sneeze, a Romeo y Julieta lit, the match extinguished between thumb and forefinger, thumb and forefinger licked, straw hat on, his trouser legs rolled up" – he "marched" (a little lopsidedly, limping as a result of the New York accident) across the damp spring grass to the elm with the split trunk, set up his easel and his little painting table and stayed there, painting, right into the evening. David Inches, the butler – "my man" – brought dinner out to him, and refilled the ice in the champagne bucket now and again. Churchill painted the landscape, which ended in a low hill not far off to the west, and from this viewpoint consisted only of grass. He painted the sky above it, and a strip of oilseed rape on the horizon. He used thinner brushes than usual; he didn't want to finish for a long time. That day, he said, savouring the memory thirty years later, he felt like a young painter trying out oils and canvas for the first time. He forgot everything around him. He forgot himself. He forgot the landscape, too. The landscape revealed to him its true being, which was hidden not beneath its surface, but in his own heart. His own heart, he realised that day, was where Plato's realm of ideas lay. Finally a friend's prophesy had come true: one day he would understand that in his heart he was a painter, and on that day he would sit down at his easel to paint, just to paint, and not to distract himself.

The picture Churchill painted during those days in early March really does differ from his others; at first glance it looks like an abstract painting. Unusually for a landscape, it is painted in portrait format, and consists of three horizontal strips of colour, the middle one significantly thinner than those above and below it. There is nothing in the colours to suggest the natural quality of a landscape. Walker Pfannholz, an expert at Sotheby's and curator of the first Churchill retrospective (which wasn't until 1987!) describes the picture in his foreword to the catalogue as Churchill's best, better than the artist himself believed, and reminiscent of Mark Rothko's colour field painting, which was only developed twenty years later.

As he was painting, a worried Clementine tiptoed up to him several times. He didn't talk when he was painting; you could *watch* him, if you liked, but there was nothing to *hear*. She studied his face. In the evenings after dinner, he made fun of the power that was playing the fool in nearby London and in the wider world, describing what he would do with Ghandi, if he had his way. There was something to hear there. Even if recently he had started holding back, not dipping his spoon so deep into history and drawing comparisons, for example, with the notorious Tipu Sultan, the eighteenth-century ruler of the Mogul Empire in Southern India, who had liked to feed citizens of the British Empire to his pet tiger. He would usually have held forth on this subject for hours, describing unimaginable cruelties, and then adding in a stage whisper that in person, this nightmarish oriental despot had been as virtuous as an angel and as peaceful as a plant – just like Mr Ghandi.

In her biography of Clementine (*Clementine Churchill*, London 1979), Mary Soames writes that Winston's inhuman level of activity was a "heavy burden" for her mother. Listening to his undoubtedly blessed monologues, in which he was undoubtedly able to incorporate the spirits of all times into a single flowing argument, deflecting or avoiding his moods, which undoubtedly had something of the genius about them, bracing herself against his depressive silences, stoically weathering his fits of rage – in short, watching this undoubtedly great life was no less difficult than living it, because there was no second life – her own – alongside it. Clementine was used to reading her husband's caprices, even when they remained "under the skin". And she could also see his quiet despair. The colour of his face revealed a great deal. Naturally pale people have a broader palette than those with greater pigmentation. Winston's skin was a translucent film through which the translation of excitement into blood-flow was immediately visible. And he didn't turn a uniform red; it was always patchy. That wasn't attractive, but it was informative, if you knew how to read his face. A reddening of the throat that gradually spread upwards, colouring his cheeks but not the area around his nose and mouth, indicated anger. When his ears were glowing but the rest of his face remained unremarkable, it was impatience; there usually followed a contemptuous remark that would silence the person who had annoyed him for the next hour. If the skin around his eyes was a deathly grey, the interpreter knew her husband was offended. A moist forehead with a bluish pallor meant exhaustion, which, while it didn't stem the flow of speech, did churn it up, so that the speaker sometimes lost himself in conditional and consecutive clauses and never found his way back to the main part of the sentence. A noticeable reddening of the lips hinted that his mood was on the point of improving, and a jolly evening lay ahead, with interludes of silliness and more alcohol than usual. She paid attention to the rhythm and the syntactical patterns of his speech, to the idiosyncratic hums and haws, which were the most reliable indicator of whether her husband was comfortable in his own skin. Gestures and facial expressions also revealed a great deal. How he walked. The angle of his neck. How much he stooped. Whether he lifted his feet enough to avoid shuffling, or if he shuffled. How shiny or dull his fingernails were. Whether the belt of his dressing gown was wound or knotted, or if the ends dragged on the floor. Clementine had accustomed herself to checking every one of these indicators at every hour of the day and night and, if necessary, taking precautions.

22

On the other hand, if the face that was so prone to blotchiness and colouration remained uniformly white for a prolonged period, it could mean that the dog had broken out of his kennel.

Clementine hid behind the elm with the split trunk and studied her husband. And for the first time, she didn't know how to read the signs. Experience told her that steady movements, without a recognisable rhythm, could also hint at a depressive mood. Winston was painting, and whistling softly to himself. Impossible: there was nothing he detested more than whistling. He was in a good mood, there was no doubt about that. She asked David Inches for his opinion. The butler, who was the second-best reader of these clues on the estate, confirmed her impression: "I've never seen him in a better mood," he said. And then he added: "But perhaps 'good' isn't precisely it, M'lady. Even-tempered, I think, is the right expression."

But Winston's face was uniformly white, and his movements were steady. And his smile was a faraway smile.

She searched the house, checking that the guns were where they should be. She found her husband's gun loaded. That didn't necessarily mean anything. She unloaded it and hid the bullets. The .32 Webley Scott revolver and the .45 Colt were in their cases, and there was nothing to suggest that anyone had touched them since her last inspection. She set her alarm clock for four in the morning; that was the time Winston went to bed. She visited him in his bedroom, lay down beside him, stroked his hairless belly, which was even broader when he was lying down, and lifted one side of his eye mask to see if he was asleep. He said nothing; merely wound a lock of her hair around his forefinger. She laid her ear on his chest. Listened. She had read that depressive or comatose people had a heartbeat like a metronome. Winston's heartbeat was regular, peaceful, and sometimes irregular. The next day she took out the medicine chest. Found nothing unusual. As she had expected. When they were young, they had often talked about suicide, in a matter-of-fact tone, as if suicide was an ethnological phenomenon, only to be observed in a particular race to which they did not belong. And they had pondered how, if they did belong to this race, they would go about it. Clementine preferred the bloodier options, while Winston favoured poison. In death, she told him, she wouldn't care about aesthetics and discretion. "Well, I do," he replied. She didn't believe him. She found the fact that he was lying to her alarming. Winston would shoot himself. He wouldn't even consider anything else. She told herself she should be shocked by such thoughts. But she wasn't shocked.

The next evening Robert J.G. Boothby and Brendan Bracken came to visit. They were both part of his regular audience. Winston called them friends. Clementine called them his regular audience – partly with the aim of detracting from their intimidating individuality. Bracken, for instance, was cultivating a hairstyle you could see from the moon. They were among the few people who had not turned away from the former Chancellor of the Exchequer after he had been forced into a corner by Stanley Baldwin. Boothby and Bracken saw Winston as the leader of the Conservative Party, whether he was officially in charge of it or not.

They stayed until long after midnight, eating the crab mayonnaise that Sir Abe Bailey had brought back from South Africa and the goose liver pâté that one of Clementine's cousins had brought back from France, drinking champagne and scotch, and listening to Winston hold forth on photography – which he did in an unusually quiet voice, leaving space for questions, leaving space for himself to think. He said that photography always reaches us in the past tense, and that makes it the saddest of all the arts: it speaks of a moment that will never return. "Painting says: *it is*; photography says: *it was*". Photography, he said, was leading painting into a crisis, just as film had done to theatre, and talking pictures to silent film. Nor was literature immune to such a crisis, he said, for who could guarantee that one day humanity wouldn't turn away from the written and back to the spoken word – what were a few thousand years of writing against hundreds of thousands of years when people would gather round to sit and listen to a man if he was eloquent enough. Everything was subject to change: every art, every office, politics, life, emotions, passions. No moment ever returned.

"I know it's a rather banal insight. But thinking it is different from understanding it. I only understood it when I thought about photography as I was painting."

This was all very, very sad. But then again it wasn't. Doing the same thing over and over again – that would be true madness.

As Clementine was seeing the guests to their car, where their chauffeur was asleep, Boothby said: "He's happy. Am I correct?"

Clementine nodded.

"So that's what he looks like when he's happy. It's a sight that takes some getting used to. Happy or contented?"

What was the difference, Clementine asked.

"I've never seen him in such a good mood," Boothby marvelled. "Is that the right expression? One can say that. Can't one?"

"Inches thinks he's even-tempered. I'd say he's right. That's better than 'in a good mood'. It lasts longer."

"And I thought politics was as addictive as opium."

"That only applies to someone who devotes his life to it," Bracken informed him, before asking Clementine: "What's he doing with himself?"

"He's painting."

"I thought that was dangerous."

"The pictures are different from what he used to paint. And he whistles while he paints."

"He whistles? Good Lord! What's he whistling?"

"*Tiptoe through the Tulips.* He hums and whistles it. First one, then the other."

"Where does he know it from?"

"Sarah sings it to him."

A great worry weighed on Clementine.

23

The first of two extant letters from Churchill to Chaplin dates from this period. Churchill alludes to the worry that was weighing on *him*, and gives the impression that of all his cares, the one that weighed heaviest was not, as all the biographies claim, concern about his loss of power in the House of Commons and the Conservative Party, or the fear that he might have reached the end of his political career and would die of boredom. Nor was it, as Clementine thought when she wrote to her sister-in-law Gwendoline of "*our* first concern" (my emphasis), anxiety about their son Randolph. And it wasn't the marriage on which Diana was embarking, with a man she didn't love – didn't even know. He was most worried about his daughter Sarah. Other sources confirm this impression. He told Brendan Bracken several times that "my mother's blood flows in Sarah's veins". Bracken knew what Winston meant by that. He mentioned it in a letter to a friend, and evidently the friend also knew what was meant by it. "Poor Sarah," the friend wrote back. "Poor Winston, poor Clementine!"

Sarah was now eighteen years old and, in her father's view, much too interested in men; Bracken describes her in his typically blunt manner as "man-mad". She was not beautiful in a conventional sense, her face was too narrow, her hair too flaming, her teeth a little too long, too white – but even as a young woman she exuded a sexual desire and a sexual allure that made men flock around her at any gathering, and she wasn't afraid to show her feelings. In this, she was like her grandmother, Jennie.

Winston's mother, Jeanette "Jennie" Churchill, née Jerome, was the daughter of an American businessman and speculator, and one of the most beautiful women of her day. She and her husband had

not been a good match, people said after his premature death: heart-
felt passion had met with an overly cool, calculating head. Arthur
James Balfour (prime minister from 1902 to 1905) characterised the
couple in a similar way: "Lord Randolph was a fanatic, and Jennie
a romantic. His passion burned up love; hers burned up reason." As
a widow, Jennie led a promiscuous life, conducting countless affairs
with men including King Edward VII, King Milan of Serbia, and
the Austrian diplomat Count Charles Kinsky. The Imperial Chancellor Otto von Bismarck, the most faithful of faithful husbands,
met her in Bad Kissingen and fell so deeply in love with Jennie,
who was forty years his junior, that he left in a mad rush before
he did "something he might regret", as he confided to his biographer Lothar Bucher. The writer and politician Lord D'Abernon,
one of the most influential European statesmen of the inter-war
years, raved about her. "More of the panther than the woman in her
look," he said, "but with a cultivated intelligence unknown to the
jungle." Prominent men were not her only conquests; there was no
element of snobbery in her sexual desire. By her own reckoning, she
had more than two hundred lovers. After the death of Winston's
father she married twice more; her last husband was twenty-five
years younger than she was, and five years younger than her son
Winston. She was sixty-six.

Winston was far from prudish; in aristocratic circles it was not
customary to link sexuality and morality too closely. He admired
his mother, writing to her at the age of twenty-four: "There is no
doubt that the two of us, you and I, are thoughtless in the same way
– spendthrift and extravagant." By the latter he meant: without "an
over-developed sense of morality". He wanted to be like his father,
and he wanted to be like his mother. But, as he concluded mourn-
fully, he lacked all the necessary qualities to be like his father, and
he lacked "the insatiable joy in life" to be like his mother, as he
put it in one of his autobiographical columns (which, like a dozen
other similar texts, he never published). The notorious vitality of

the "Renaissance man" was not joy in life, but, as he writes in the same place, a "discipline against death". The truth was: sexuality repulsed him – though not in a bourgeois, moralistic sense. He even tolerated braggarts, though he himself had an almost monk-like existence. He remembered his mother as a driven woman; the "insatiable joy" he spoke of was a euphemism. He knew she was unhappy; she suffered from her desires as from an addiction. And he also knew that she had considered taking her own life no less often than he had.

When he first employed his very private private secretary, William Knott, he told him: "I weep a terrible great deal. You will have to get used to it." When he thought about his father, he often started to cry – and when he thought about his mother, he always did.

He was afraid his daughter Sarah might fall prey to the same addiction as his mother. The fact that, like her brother, she was drinking excessively before she had even reached the age of twenty, didn't trouble him; the fact that she couldn't look at a man without everyone knowing what was on her mind, did.

This makes his letter to Chaplin all the more surprising. Of course, Winston was aware of his friend's reputation in Hollywood, and beyond. After all, when they had first met, some very ugly allegations were being made against Chaplin, and the newspapers were spreading the most scandalous rumours.

There isn't a single letter from Churchill in the papers Chaplin left behind, nor is there a letter from Chaplin in Churchill's. However, two "drafts" were found among Churchill's papers. I place the term in inverted commas because it is impossible to tell whether these really are drafts, or finished letters that simply weren't sent – or sent in another form, and subsequently destroyed by the recipient. The letter I am talking about here was produced on a typewriter – a surprising fact, because if Churchill wrote at all, as opposed to giving dictation, then it was always by hand. Considering the letter's content, we can rule out the possibility that he dictated it to a secretary who typed it up from her shorthand. William Knott says that – for whatever reason – Churchill typed the letter himself, and as evidence of this he cites the many typographical errors – which I have corrected here.

(I found the letter among my father's documents, a copy of a copy of a copy, faint and barely legible in places. William Knott sent him the pages at his entreaties, but only after extracting from him a promise not to quote so much as a single sentence from them, no matter where. The promise wouldn't have been necessary; my father was a discreet man. His interest in the letter-writer was different to mine – although we could have chosen the same title for this interest: *Saving the World*. But I was more preoccupied with the question of how, before saving the world, the saviour had saved himself, and from what. And there is no sense in being discreet here. No, I drag everything out into the light. When I come home late at night after my performances, my wife routinely asks: "You've smashed everything again, haven't you?" and I routinely reply: "Yes. Yes. Yes.")

Dear Charlie,
My daughter Sarah has just been in to see me. She visited me in my study. She often has trouble sleeping. She is terribly downhearted. She wants to become an actress. She told me she has already auditioned for several theatres. I didn't know. She acted in a play at just sixteen. I didn't know. It was a small role in an unimportant play in a small theatre. She auditioned and they liked her. She gave them a false name and date of birth. But the truth came out. The impresario wanted to have new posters made up with her real name and mine – my name twice the size of hers. He was expecting a full house and a long run. But Sarah refused. So he dismissed her.
She says that acting is her life. She says she hates the name Churchill because it's ruining her life. She says that in England, the daughter of Winston Churchill is never going to be judged on what she is, and what she is capable of. She wept. I told her that the Americans have

no prejudices, neither aristocratic nor plebeian; they're pragmatists. I told her about you, Charlie. Take Charlie Chaplin, I said, he was among the poorest of the poor, at the bottom end of the lower classes, he stood no chance in England, just as you stand no chance for the opposite reason. I was so very moved by her anguish! I'm sure you understand. I said: try your luck in America. I believe I managed to console her. She is brimming with plans. Perhaps, after the great general and statesman Marlborough, the Churchills are destined to produce a great actress, just as all the Chaplins before you, Charlie, were destined to produce the Tramp. I told her: people won't say, that's Winston Churchill's daughter; they'll say, that's Sarah Churchill's father. They'll say it in America first, and then all over the world, and one day they'll say it in England, too.

In days gone by parents chose wives for their sons and husbands for their daughters. And that was all right. I can find no reason to deviate from this custom. In days gone by the barriers between the classes were insurmountable, and that was all right. Today, hard work and success count for something, and that is better.

Do you remember our evening, the three of us, at the Biltmore? Sarah was so entranced by you! You, Charlie, are a man who is forever young, because as a child you were older than other children. You need a passionate young woman by your side, with knowledge of your vocation. Sarah brings everything with her to guarantee a happy match. Let your heart decide, but first listen to the arguments of reason, the heart's secretary.

Sarah will travel to the United States, to the country of her grandmother's birth. I am worried for her. Protect her, Charlie! I do not need to mention that I am in your debt to the end of my days, but I would like to say that there is nothing I would rather be than your debtor.

Yours,
Winston

24

On top of everything else, he was an author. He was a third of the way through his biography of John Churchill, the first Duke of Marlborough; he had promised the publisher two hundred thousand words, and it looked like it was going to be a lot more (in the end, it would be five times as many). The advance was the highest that had ever been paid in the history of English publishing, but it didn't even cover his expenses. Three secretaries stood ready to work at all times, taking dictation in shifts. A doctoral student from Oxford marshalled half a dozen students to search for sources in public and private libraries; Churchill never used a document without checking it himself for credibility and importance. "His historical knowledge was boundless," as Martin Gilbert, one of England's leading historians, said simply.

How are we to explain the fact that sensible people who knew Churchill well – unlike Hitler, who *didn't* know him – described him as workshy, at the very least? (Hitler insulted him from Berlin, calling him a "drunkard and a laggard of the first order".) How are we to explain the fact that he never shook off a reputation for being dissolute, a charlatan, a pretender, an also-ran? How are we to explain the fact that even the greatest recognition bestowed upon him lacked warmth? My father was so taken by these questions he wrote an essay on the subject. It is one of numerous essays he wrote about Winston Churchill, most of which were never published. Some were, though this was the only one that appeared in an international journal, *The English Historical Review*. Doubtless William Knott put in a good word for him; the *EHR* has printed precisely three articles by German authors over the course of its hundred-year history. The title was: "Good-For-Nothing or Saviour. Work and Mission in the Lives of Churchill and Hitler". The essay was lauded and quoted at length in *The Times*. A back-translation into German was published in the *Vierteljahreshefte für Zeitgeschichte*, with a foreword by the German-American historian Hans Roth-fels. My father writes that Churchill radiated such a strong aura of conviction in his metaphysical destiny that people's expectations of him could never be fulfilled, not even by a god-like being – which naturally led to disappointment. As a mirror image to the expecta-tions which raised him to a supernatural level, the disappointment dragged perceptions of him downwards into the banal. With Hitler, it was the other way round. The whole world knew he came from an uneducated family, was a failed artist, rejected by the Academy in Vienna, and until just a few years before he was deified as the mighty Führer, had been residing in a men's hostel. Expectations were low, and the surprise therefore all the greater. The way both men were judged was founded on a hope of salvation that prob-ably arose from and continued to be driven by the dismal economic and political situation, though for the ultimate cause, we must look to the (shocking) absence of any transcendent interpretation of the modern world. Both men had become the focus of this hope of salvation. In Churchill's case, the words were: *We have a saviour among us*; in Hitler's, they were: *We have been sent a saviour*. The first phrase strengthened the British belief in one's own power, one's own people, one's own nation; the second strengthened a belief in what Hitler himself called "providence". A saviour who is not much different from you and I enjoys only transient trust; salvation sent from a metaphysical realm, on the other hand, is absolute. Demo-cratic elections in 1945 put an end to Churchill's career as a saviour; Hitler himself put an end to his, through suicide.

Spring 1932 – the Churchill family was on holiday, travelling across the Netherlands and heading south up the Rhine, to Hesse and

Bavaria. For little Mary, Germany was a strange, fairy-tale country where grandmothers were eaten by wolves. For Clementine, Sarah, Diana and Diana's fiancé, it was *terra incognita*; they knew more about Australia, Newfoundland, the Falkland Islands or the Sudan. Any associations they could make with this country were not good ones; they were coloured by war and a stupid monarch who was, embarrassingly, related to their own royal family. Whenever their eyes met, Sarah smiled at her father with the full weight of her eighteen years, which charmed (and depressed) him. At home, she had rummaged in her father's library until she found a book containing a picture of Wilhelm II. That was how she imagined Germany, she said: stupid and ugly and pompous. But Sarah was the one who let out cries of delight as they sailed up the Rhine, past the vineyards to the Lorelei rocks. She had never seen such a beautiful landscape, she sighed. She asked if somebody could get her a book of German poetry; she wanted to learn some off by heart, even if she didn't understand a word of it. She had drawn conclusions about the German landscape from the face of the Kaiser, and now she was drawing conclusions about German poetry from the landscape. Her mother told her she was much too old for such nonsense, and in any case German was a language splintered with consonants, like the battlefield at the Somme. It was not beautiful. But Sarah was determined, and Winston was on her side.

At Koblenz they left the ship and continued their journey in a special carriage attached to a Reichsbahn train. They spent a few days in Blindheim, Swabia. In August 1704, it had been the site of the famous Battle of Blenheim, the decisive encounter between the armies of John Churchill and Prince Eugene of Savoy on one side, and the French troops of King Louis XIV and Elector Maximilian II Emanuel's Bavarian soldiers on the other. Why not make use of the holiday to visit the former battlefields of the Duke's campaign? Winston had studied the battle at home, and with every detail imprinted on his mind, he could now lecture on location. He had convinced Frederick Lindemann, an old friend of the family known as "the Prof", to join them for at least part of the holiday. Lindemann was a professor of experimental physics at Oxford University, and an icon of sanity. He advised Churchill on matters of military technology – and he spoke German and enjoyed acting as interpreter. He insisted on purchasing a volume of German ballads in a bookshop in Stuttgart, and handed it to Sarah with a straight face. This permanently sullen man who always smelled of ambergris, and obstinately maintained the Bohemian tradition of scorning any kind of audience, taught her with the "patience of a donkey" (this was the German expression for it, he said), what the words meant and how they were pronounced. Sarah learned Heinrich Heine's "Loreley", the "Erlkönig" by Goethe, "Die Bürgschaft" by Schiller, and Ludwig Uhland's "Der gute Kamerad". From then on, half an hour after dinner in the hotel was reserved for her recitations. Before she started, she would tell them what each ballad was about. These were the most pleasant evenings of the trip, her father would tell his very private private secretary years later, his delight still evident even then. The second verse of "Der gute Kamerad" moved him to tears every time. And the prime minister would close his eyes and recite – in German:

> A musket ball comes flying,
> Is it meant for him or me?
> It cuts him down, and dying,
> At my feet he's lying,
> Just like a part of me.

And William Knott would say: "You are a warrior, sir."
And Winston Churchill would reply: "That is my vocation."

25

Another warrior: his ancestor, John Churchill. He had a bad reputation, despite having saved Europe from the tyranny of a megalomaniac. In the chronicles of the nation, the Earl of Marlborough was painted as a man you couldn't rely on, a man you could just as easily imagine fighting for the other side, the evil side. And as the historians remembered it, he had in fact spun his intrigues on that side, for a little while at least. Ever since he was a boy, Winston had felt at once attracted and repelled by this character.

John went to court as a page at fifteen. The king took a liking to him, advanced his career, kept him close, and finally offered him his friendship. James II wanted England to return to Catholicism, and he wanted to become an absolute monarch in the French mould. But his daughter Mary and her husband, William III of Orange, had powerful friends who organised an uprising, toppled the king and drove him into exile in France. John Churchill, the protégé, wasn't at his king's side, but in the rebels' ranks.

Nobody loves a traitor, not even a traitor acting in the country's best interests. But he might still be forgiven by later generations, if among their historians he finds a skilful defender who discerns a tragic struggle between friendship and patriotic duty behind his betrayal. But if he commits treason a second time, nobody will care about his motives. The art of rhetoric, be it his own or his defence counsel's, will be no help to him then. And John Churchill did commit treason again, this time against William of Orange. He reportedly wrote a letter to his former master during the latter's exile in France, warning him of an attack on the French fleet at Brest.

But Winston had discovered that this portentous letter didn't exist: the only copy was a forgery, and he could prove it. Even the historians who opposed him (in the guild, he was seen as a cock-sure dilettante, another Heinrich Schliemann, except that he wasn't claiming to have found Troy) had to admit he was right. Finally he was permitted to speak out and show his hero as he had wanted to see him since he was a boy. John Churchill, his ancestor, was neither an opportunist nor a scoundrel on the make. He was a clever, pragmatic politician. And he was on the right side. He led the English army against Louis XIV. He saved Europe from the worst kind of tyranny.

Winston dictated the foreword to the first volume of his Marlborough biography while he was visiting the battlefield at Blenheim, outside in the April sun:

In 1688 Europe drew swords in a quarrel which [...] was to last for a quarter of a century. Since the duel between Rome and Carthage there had been no such world war. It involved all the civilized peoples; it extended to every part of the accessible globe; it settled for some time or permanently the relative wealth and power, and the frontiers of almost every European state.

The first volume of *Marlborough: His Life and Times* was published in 1933 – the same year Adolf Hitler became German Chancellor.

Churchill dictated for at least two hours a day – outdoors whenever possible. The secretaries were busy with things other than listening to him – namely writing – but he still required an audience for his off-the-cuff speeches, even if it consisted of just two ears and two eyes, so friends and family members took turns to listen. After just a few days of this, they began to duck out. And finally, ten-year-old Mary was the only one left. She loved nothing better than listening to her father. And he liked nothing better than telling her about her long-ago ancestors. He could see Mary looking at history as if she were leafing through a picture book, and he came to look at history like Mary. He dictated calmly and steadily, directing his words into the hand and pencil of his secretary "Mrs P.", and the wide eyes of his daughter.

Many years later he wrote a column in *The Times* about these afternoons: first of all, he said, the girl made him express himself in terms she could understand; and secondly, she made him emphasise the narrative and hold back on the ruminations. Following this experience he re-wrote the previous chapters, and if critics today (he penned these thoughts after he had been awarded the Nobel Prize) praised the fact that his Marlborough biography (for which it had been awarded) read like an exciting novel, then this was thanks to none other than his daughter Mary, who had always asked the right questions, and who was less interested in *history* than in *the story*. "World history, as bombastic as it sometimes appears, is merely the scenery before which one person, or two, or half a dozen, live a part of their lives. One can only tell the stories of individuals; history as a whole cannot be told." He wanted to use this – a quote from his own article – as the motto at the start of his six-volume *History of the Second World War* (published in 1954), but he left it out after a friend – Frederick Lindemann, in fact – warned him that wicked tongues might say the book should actually have been called: *Me, Against the Backdrop of the Second World War.*

The Marlborough biography was "too successful" according to Rilana Jamchy, who was the features editor of the Israeli daily newspaper *Haaretz* in the early seventies. But she wasn't talking about the book's literary quality. You could see Louis XIV as Hitler, she said. The Sun King had been made to serve as a prototype for that singular mass-butcher. In truth, she said, the biography was not an academic work of history, but a *roman à clef*. What nonsense, considering when the book was written – the whole thing completed before the outbreak of war, and a third of it before Hitler even took power! But true nonetheless. John Churchill is Winston; the Frenchman is the Austrian.

Ms Jamchy was not the first to remark on the fact that this book was the scene of a *battle before the battle*. As early as 1959, the Danish psychoanalyst Eskild Ottensen wrote that here we have "one of the most remarkable anachronisms in modern literature", an unusual anachronism that didn't turn back time, but turned it forwards. Churchill's Marlborough biography reminded him of Palaeolithic cave paintings, depicting animals that were yet to be hunted. Ottensen believed he had discovered an unsettling vein of magical thinking running through all the statesman's works – literary and pictorial. He saw evidence that Churchill had no feeling for symbols. He recounts the anecdote from Winston's swearing-in as President of the Board of Trade by Edward VII in 1908, when in all seriousness he reassured those present that he wasn't intending to do the king harm; the latter had appeared not only in an ermine robe and a crown, but carrying a sceptre, and evidently the new minister saw it not as a symbol, but as the cudgel from which the royal utensil doubtless originated. Ottensen speaks of this as a defect, though he emphasises that Churchill certainly didn't lack the capacity for abstract thought; that would be tantamount to describing him as stupid, which of course he was not. He called this defect "Churchill Syndrome". Nor does it surprise him, he writes, that the young Winston was a truant. In the early years of education, children are taught and must practise symbolic thinking above all: digits, numbers, letters. It was no wonder that Churchill was thrown off balance by the vocative and its requirement that he address a table. In the story of the First Duke of Marlborough and his fight against Louis XIV, Churchill symbolically pre-empted his own fight against Hitler. Writing the book was already part of this battle, although logically, when he was writing it, he couldn't have predicted whether the fight would actually take place. That was Eskild Ottensen's theory.

In my father's opinion, very few of the people who speculated on Churchill as a writer had actually read the *Marlborough*. He, too, saw the work as a novel: one of the most significant novels of the century, a thing like *War and Peace*, like Stendhal's *Charterhouse of Parma*. William Knott concurred: Sir Winston, he wrote in one of his letters, had liked it when people referred to his book as a novel – though admittedly, he added, somebody first had to explain to him how much broader the term "novel" had become in the twentieth century. Churchill's literary tastes had been "modest", said Knott, confined to C.S. Forester's *Hornblower* novels and Winwood Reade's *The Martyrdom of Man*, and of course he loved Walter Scott and James Fenimore Cooper, whom he considered the most important American novelist. But at the same time he had poured scorn on contemporary novel-writers, who clearly had no new ideas and were still writing like Forester, Reade, Scott and Cooper. When Knott suggested to him that this accusation was entirely wrong with regard to modern literature, and mentioned names like James Joyce, Marcel Proust or William Faulkner, his boss would dismiss it with a wave of his hand – how good could these people be if he had never heard of them? Knott closed this chapter by saying that of all the Nobel Literature laureates, Churchill had certainly been the one with the least literary education.

Of course one should believe that Winston Churchill identified strongly with the hero of his "novel", John Churchill. One should believe that, firstly, he was fighting to clear his name; secondly, that he was a shadow from posterity fighting at his ancestor's side against the French despot; and thirdly, that this fight was a symbolic *battle before the battle* against another adversary, who had already started to cause trouble when Churchill was writing, cobbling together a bunch of desperados – the fanatical, the bloodline-obsessed and the just plain stupid – into a party called the NSDAP, which was to form the core of the outfit he would use to try and get the better of Germany and then the world. Before, during and after the awarding of the Nobel Prize in 1953, when people kept on and on telling Churchill that the *Marlborough* was a unique example of political prophesy, he never showed the weakness of trying to play the comparison down – yes, he found it incredible too, he said, but that was just how he saw it: he was the Duke, and the Duke was him.

My father collected everything to do with the protagonist of his research, which meant he also read various biographies of Louis XIV. He searched through the memoirs of the Duc de Saint-Simon and the Cardinal of Retz, read the letters of Liselotte von der Pfalz, immersed himself in Harrison Salter's weighty monograph on the period and, not least, studied *The Sun King* by Nancy Mitford, Clementine Churchill's cousin, where he saw all kinds of things written between the lines. He finally formed a picture of the King of France that shocked him deeply. But this shock didn't relate to the absolutist monarch himself; it concerned a fact that nobody had yet picked up on – certainly not Churchill himself.

Naturally, Churchill wanted to identify with the hero of his novel, the First Duke of Marlborough. He wanted to be like him.

But he wasn't like the Duke.

John Churchill is quite a different character. One can, one *must* see him as the antithesis of the author. Though in this context, it doesn't matter who John Churchill really was. The important thing is how his descendant and biographer Winston Churchill painted him. Who Louis XIV really was matters just as little. But the person on whom the novelist Winston Churchill based the despot is a truly astounding choice.

Louis XIV may be a distant reflection of A.H., but first and foremost he is a perfect self-portrait of his author W.C.!

This was my father's conclusion. He wrote an essay on the subject for the *Blättern für Geschichte und Politik*, issue 2, 1979.

Did Churchill ever recognise that he had portrayed himself in the Sun King? My father didn't believe so. In Marc Landier's brilliant study *Through the Looking-Glass: Churchill's Doppelganger*, the Belgian-British historian and philosopher put forward the theory that Churchill was the first (and for a long time the only) person to see through Hitler, because he was similar to him in many ways – which made my father crow triumphantly, in his "English" manner, by raising an eyebrow, underlining the paragraph with a pencil, taking off his glasses and slowly sliding the journal across the kitchen table towards me.

"Landier should have quoted you," I said. "Or at least mentioned you."

My father curled his lips into a smile and gave a barely perceptible shake of his head.

26

> All Wednesday afternoon I spent flying round with Hitler from one meeting to another. First of all we lunched at the aerodrome just outside Berlin. Hitler is a teetotaller, a non-smoker and a vegetarian. On this occasion he ate his favourite scrambled eggs and salads. His lieutenants and I fortify ourselves with a more substantial meal.

So said an article in the London *Sunday Graphic* on 31 July 1932, the day of the German parliamentary elections. The reporter was Randolph Churchill, who was just twenty-one years old.

Randolph was one of half a dozen foreign journalists who accompanied Hitler on his election campaign tour. Did Hitler know whose son this young man was? Goebbels knew. It's possible he kept it from his Führer. The propagandist might well have regarded accrediting the young man as a cunning trick, which would pay off at some point. But he also thought he knew that Hitler didn't agree with playing off the cushion and shied away from intrigue. Though at the same time – and this is the refrain in his diaries – Goebbels believed it was "almost a law of nature" that the Führer's charisma would win all hearts and minds; he could therefore be confident that Randolph would write an article sympathetic to the movement. A report in an English newspaper that contained even cautious praise, and was signed by a Churchill, no matter which one, was still worth more than ten enthusiastic articles by a Mills, a Jones or a Brown.

Randolph was a man of many talents, with a dazzling exterior. "He looks like a Greek god," gushed Ann-Mari von Bismarck, wife of the German ambassador, though she added – and this is seldom quoted – "and behaves like a satyr." He was brilliant, arrogant, cynical, a know-it-all who actually did know it all most of the time, and who certainly knew how to have the last laugh. He had a talent for creating an audience and turning that audience into his accomplices when he wanted to humiliate a third party. He was a winner, successful with women and busy making an international career for himself as an author and journalist. He admired his father, and although he smoked cigarettes, he imitated him in everything else.

In truth, he was completely clueless about the great man. He knew nothing about depression – nothing in general, and nothing about the illness in his family. If somebody had enlightened him, he would have dismissed it: his father was too strong, too powerful, too influential, too brilliant to let himself be ruled by an insubstantial thing like the soul. In a letter to his son, Churchill uses the following revealing words: "If, as I'm sure you meant to, and forgot, you had asked me how things were at home, I would have replied: life is flowing peacefully downstream."

Randolph had a vested interest in his father making a political comeback. Unlike his sister Sarah, he liked to let the sun of the Churchills shine on him. He had come up with a potential non-parliamentary role for his father that would give the family name more weight – more than all the enervating detail-work in the House of Commons and his many committees and sub-committees put together. He didn't think the future of Europe was generally decided in its parliaments. He thought the future of the world would be decided by a few great men. His father was one of these great men. Adolf Hitler was another.

In Munich, he had made friends with Ernst Hanfstaengl, Hitler's foreign policy advisor, the man who had introduced the Führer to high society and, as he boasted, taught him some proper manners. Hanfstaengl, a giant of a man with the flat face of a boxer – paradoxically, he was known as "Putzi" (baby) – had grown up in New York, where his family ran an art gallery. He had studied at

Harvard, spoke several languages, had a passable singing voice and played the piano. He had an American wife, a National Socialist to her marrow, who, as people who were close to Hanfstaengl whispered, had a "mystical" connection to the Führer. Randolph was immune to any kind of ideology; Nazism left him cold. But he was interested in the man who until recently had been dipping bread in cabbage soup in a men's hostel in Vienna, and whose proletarian head was now wreathed with Germany's hopes and visions for the future. Through the Hanfstaengls he made contact with Goebbels, and through Goebbels he made contact with Hitler.

Hanfstaengl had spent some time in London, and was aware of Churchill. His opinion: though the man was approaching sixty, and looked his age, looked like an old has-been, he was the only politician in Europe with enough guts, character, ambition and vigour to plan the old continent anew with Hitler: a Europe in which Germany and England weren't enemies; where they had a mutual respect, the Germans respecting England as a leading naval force, the English respecting Germany as the only real power on the continent. Together, they would be a bulwark against Bolshevism. Hitler admired, almost venerated the British Empire, and had always wanted to come to some arrangement with England, as Hanfstaengl had always advised him. So far, Churchill hadn't said anything negative about the Führer and National Socialism – in fact, he had even made some positive comments – and he had spoken out against Poincaré in 1922, in favour of a policy of communication with Germany. Hanfstaengl was delighted with Randolph's idea. The international community would be relieved to learn that – as Randolph phrased it in a circular to selected journalists – "finally we have real experts with the chutzpah to address this hopeless-looking situation and do some straight talking with each other." Another word would have to be found for "chutzpah" in the German press release – Hanfstaengl insisted on it.

Before the start of the Churchill family's trip through Holland

and Germany, Randolph had telephoned his father, who said he was prepared to meet Hitler for a "private dinner". Hanfstaengl, meanwhile, had spoken to Hitler, and obtained his agreement as well. They settled on Munich as the location for the meeting. And so Hanfstaengl reserved the splendid private dining room at the Hotel Continental on Max-Joseph-Straße, and ordered a supper for eleven people.

27

Ernst and Helene Hanfstaengl arrived at eight o'clock, an hour late – without Hitler. They apologised for Hitler's lateness, and their own (they had been waiting for him themselves): the election campaign was in full swing, and the Führer was conducting a campaign like no politician had ever done before. He was flying from one city to the next, sometimes appearing at three events in one day, in front of ten thousand people, in Dortmund in the afternoon, Cologne in the early evening, and Berlin later the same night, speaking for one to two hours in each place. He never spoke on the same topic twice in a row, but his "ineffable" enthusiasm never wavered.

They waited.

At nine, when Hitler still wasn't there, Clementine suggested starting dinner.

Helene Hanfstaengl seemed amused by the Führer's rudeness – in the same way some doting mothers, convinced their sons are unique, will view their bad behaviour as evidence of this uniqueness. She told them how she and her dear friends Helene Bechstein and Elsa Bruckmann, the former the wife of the piano manufacturer, the latter born Princess Cantacuzène, had tried to teach him how to behave properly. "It's like telling a hurricane to blow gently." A full silver-service dinner, attending a concert, a fitting with the tailor, how to address various ranks of the nobility, the correct use of commas, various conversational styles for use with diplomats, academics, conductors, captains of industry.

"The man is an idea," she said, moving her head slowly from one side to the other, as if – Sarah recalled later – she was trying to indicate the breadth of this idea, and looking down at the table as she did so. She said again: "The man is an idea."

There was a grand piano in the room: "a Bechstein, naturally." Hanfstaengl played a potpourri of the music Hitler loved – Johann Strauss, Liszt, Brahms – and some old Scottish dances. He turned the announcement of each piece into a little sketch. He mimicked Goebbels, Göring, Kaiser Wilhelm II – he didn't do Mussolini because Herr Hitler was better at that, he said, though he did send up the former US president Woodrow Wilson by, in his words, performing all actions an inch to one side of where he meant to. Surely his best impression would be Frankenstein's monster, Randolph called out. He was treating the giant like a hired entertainer. But the object of his ridicule laughed along with him, telling the party that Herr Hitler always said the same thing. And his wife, who was laughing too, said that the monster was the good guy in the novel; the villain was Doctor Frankenstein, which of course was why he was called Frankenstein. At which Professor Lindemann asked if she meant to imply that Mary Shelley chose the name Frankenstein for the evil scientist because she believed it was a Jewish name. And Frau Hanfstaengl replied, without looking at the Prof, without looking at anyone, that she knew all the Jewish names, really, all of them, including the ones that sounded particularly German, and she could smell Jewish skin even through perfumed tweed.

"And I can smell death," Winston butted in. It was the first thing he had said all evening. "It stinks like brewed yellow shit." He was deeply shocked at himself – he couldn't believe he had just said such a thing, and on top of that so loudly, so belligerently – and his wife and children were shocked, too.

But Frau Hanfstaengl nodded, and as the colour drained from Winston's face, he was the only one she looked at.

"I'm just the same, Mr Churchill," she said gently. "I can smell it, and I sense its presence." She told the story of how, on 10 November 1923, after the failed Beer Hall Putsch, she had prevented Hitler from taking his own life by twisting the gun from his hand with a jiu-jitsu grip and burying it in a barrel of flour.

A silence fell over the room.

To break it, Herr Hanfstaengl suggested that Sarah recite a German poem, since she had told him that this was her new passion, and he would improvise to it on the piano.

That evening, Sarah recited "Die Bürgschaft" by Friedrich Schiller, Churchill remembered – it had to be this poem, this most German of all German poems, in which a brutal tyrant learns the value of friendship – and the giant with the ingratiating demeanor and the concave face of an imbecile tinkled away to it, much too loudly, much too clumsily, without any feeling for the delicate quality of her voice.

After her father's death, William Knott spoke to Sarah Churchill about that evening, keen to hear the detail of the incident. She remembered it, though she thought it had been a different poem – not "Die Bürgschaft", certainly not "Die Bürgschaft". Although, she said, it was typical of her father to dramatize reality in hindsight: the saviour of the world waiting for the destroyer of the world, a monster at the piano, the gentle virgin reciting a poem, and the whole scene playing out in Germany – it could only have been "Die Bürgschaft".

28

In one of his letters, William Knott told my father that two years after Churchill's death, he had been invited to Chartwell by Mary, now Mrs Soames, to help her and the historian Martin Gilbert go through her father's correspondence. By this point, said Knott, the family had known for some time of the role he had played in Churchill's life during the war. Lady Churchill had truly valued his services, if what he had done as "secretary to her husband's soul" could be described as a service; she had even suggested paying him a life annuity, an offer he had declined. His task, as William Knott told Lady Churchill in reply, had been to serve a man; but if one considered the times in which this service was rendered, and to *which* man, it had also been a service to mankind, and one should not accept payment for such a thing. In any case – so Knott wrote to my father – when it came to ordering Churchill's correspondence for publication, the family decided to seek his advice. Mrs Soames offered him the role of joint editor. This he also declined; he appreciated the honour and was keen to help, but he still had no desire to appear in the public gaze.

Thus he set off for Chartwell and stayed there for almost three months – being treated like a member of the family, making friends with the dogs, the ducks and the swans, picking vegetables and frequently cooking for the whole party. He conducted long conversations with Mrs Churchill in particular who, if he might blow his own trumpet, placed the greatest trust in him. And he drank some of the whisky left by Sir Winston – not a pretentious single malt, just Johnnie Walker Red Label. They worked for up to ten hours a day. Knott, Mrs Soames, and that nice young man Martin Gilbert divided up the bundles between them, around twenty large crates altogether. Churchill hadn't been a great believer in filing, and each of them was faced with a great variety of important and unimportant, personal and political, published and "secret" letters. In one of his crates, Knott writes, there were two letters that made his heart beat faster. Both were addressed to Mr Charles Chaplin.

I have quoted the first in full.

The second letter is "queer and troubling and ghastly" – to such a degree that William Knott decided to keep this document from his former master's relatives. I think he meant Randolph above all; he feared that the dandy, who had always hated him and tried to humiliate him at every opportunity, had now become "a dangerous, unpredictable Robin Goodfellow" who would get up to some mischief with it, whatever that might mean.

This is William Knott's description of what he found: a sheet of strong, white paper, six feet long and just as wide, made from two pieces stuck together. It was found tightly rolled inside a cardboard tube, open at the top and bottom, and is covered in words written in dark brown ink. The writing runs in a spiral, starting at the outside and working inwards. We may imagine that Churchill lay face-down on the paper and turned as he wrote. The writing becomes wobbly and erratic due to the uncomfortable writing position, which must have become more and more uncomfortable the closer the spiral of words came to the writer's body. At the centre is a circular stain, around twelve inches in diameter. William Knott believes it is a sweat patch. Churchill was inclined to perspire. William Knott believes he was naked as he wrote. Evidently Churchill had recalled Chaplin's method of battling the black dog – the *method of the clown*.

Before Churchill embarked on his spiral, he wrote a kind of preamble in the top left-hand corner of the sheet:

Dear Friend!
Charlie,
I cling to my childish beliefs: there is nothing that cannot be touched, and what cannot be touched does not exist. You can touch the skin of the dying man, you can feel it growing colder.

In the spiral, Churchill gives a succinct description of the evening with the Hanfstaengls in the Hotel Continental.

At one point that evening, he writes, he left the *séparée* to wash his face and get some fresh air. In the lavatories, he encountered a man. At first he only saw him from behind. The man was about to have a shave; he had pulled his suit jacket down off his shoulders, to his forearms, and was bending over the wash basin. His cheeks, mouth, chin and throat were covered in a thick layer of shaving foam. Churchill nodded at the man's reflection in the mirror, and the greeting was returned. And just then, the man cut himself with the razor, between his ear and his temple. The cut was obviously deep; the shaving foam on his cheek turned red in seconds. What happened next, Churchill writes, was something he had previously lacked the courage to put into words. The man started to curse, in a foreign language "splintered with consonants", brandishing his razor at his mirror image as he did so – and Churchill let himself be infected by it, just as he had with Mrs Everest when he was a little boy, and joined in the cursing. And because there was nobody in the room but the two of them, and neither understood the other's language, meaning they could be neither astonished nor offended by each other's curses, they soon gave up on real words and lapsed into a gibberish that all men on earth understood, as if they had been born before Babylon, and soon they also stopped looking in the mirror and into the reflection of each other's eyes, or their own. They turned round, and each of them, wild-eyed, cursed straight at the world – until they had had enough, and Churchill turned and hurried out.

With that, Churchill's spiral reached his belly; the rest, William Knott wrote to my father, is smudged and illegible.

29

But that is not the end of the story. At the age of eighty, Ernst Hanfstaengl wrote his memoirs (*Zwischen Weißem und Braunen Haus. Memoiren eines politischen Außenseiters*, Munich, 1970). His book also mentions the evening in the Hotel Continental in April 1932. He says how awkward the situation had been for him. He had tried several times to reach Hitler, as he writes:

> I went to the hotel phone booths and called first the Brown House and then Hitler's private apartment. Both times I was told the same thing: nobody could say where Hitler was to be found. A second later, I thought I was hallucinating: on the staircase before me I saw Hitler, still unshaven and wearing his threadbare trench-coat. I rushed towards him and hissed: 'For God's sake, Herr Hitler, what are you doing here? Churchill or his son could show up at any moment.' Hitler replied that unshaven, and in this attire, he couldn't and wouldn't [meet them].

Hanfstaengl goes on to say that he advised Hitler to borrow a fresh shirt from the hotel, have a shave and come to the private dining room. The Churchills were nice people, they would forgive his lateness, and it could still be a pleasant evening. He was sure he didn't need to remind Hitler how important this meeting was. But Hitler declined. And Hanfstaengl was left with no option but to convey this message – though admittedly without mentioning that he had seen Herr Hitler.

Of course, William Knott was familiar with Ernst Hanfstaengl's book. My father had read it too. Both found it repellent, pretentious, megalomaniacal and sycophantic at once. And both were fascinated by the thought that the man in the lavatories might have been Adolf Hitler. If it was him, then Churchill didn't recognise him. If he had recognised him, he would have been sure to mention it in his "clown letter" to Chaplin. In his memoir *The Second World War* he merely says – and his memory corroborates Hanfstaengl's – that he and his family waited in vain. He summarises: "Thus Hitler lost his only chance of meeting me. Later on, when he was all-powerful, I was to receive several invitations from him. But by that time a lot had happened, and I excused myself."

But that still isn't the end of the story.

Elsewhere I have already mentioned Erica Southern and her *Interview With the Tramp*. I know the book is frowned upon, and not just by Chaplin scholars; and God knows there are reasons enough for that. It turns the artist into the subject of gossip and tittle-tattle – which probably wouldn't have bothered Chaplin – but in so doing, it has him say things that are shockingly stupid and so clumsily phrased that a gullible reader might ask himself how this man could possibly have become what he became. The facts soon came to light: first, that Erica Southern was a pseudonym, and the author was one Lilian Bosshart; and second, that this woman had invented three quarters of Chaplin's "answers". Bosshart – and Chaplin would certainly have liked this – was a waitress at the Grand Hotel du Lac in Vevey, and occasionally looked after the table where the maestro dined with his family and guests. She had pricked up her ears and cobbled her "interview" together from what she had overheard.

Even with all these caveats, the book does give us a few interesting pieces of information. Winston Churchill is mentioned at one point. Chaplin recalls the English statesman telling him how he met a friend of Hitler's in the early thirties, who claimed the Führer had confided in her that he had wanted to commit suicide at the age of six. Chaplin replied to his friend – and I quote: "Winston, I'm afraid we can't choose the members of our club."

When I read that, the pencil slipped from my hand. William Knott gives the same quote in his letter to my father! Though here, it's Churchill who says it – word for word! Churchill told Chaplin that when he got back to the private dining room, he found Frau Hanfstaengl there alone. The children, she told him, had gone into town, and her husband had offered to drive Clementine, Mary and Professor Lindemann to the Hotel Regina – he would come back afterwards. Frau Hanfstaengl, Churchill said, was quite drunk. She reeled off the story about saving Hitler's life "by twisting the pistol from his hand with a jiu-jitsu grip and burying it in a barrel of flour" for a second time. And then she told him how that evening, she had rocked the weeping man in her arms and stroked his hair. As the gendarmes were hammering on the door, he said in a tremulous voice that he had wanted to take his own life at the age of six: day after day, his father had subjected him to savage beatings, and never missed an opportunity to ridicule him and show him up in front of other people. Churchill's comment to William Knott: "I'm afraid we can't choose the members of our club."

I don't know how this sentence reached Chaplin; but Erica Southern / Lilian Bosshart's *Interview* proves that it *did* reach him. Maybe Churchill showed his friend the "clown letter" at one of their meetings after the war. But there was only one person to whom it could have been addressed: Charlie Chaplin. Only he could have known what kind of club it was.

After this, I watched *The Great Dictator* again, and at least two scenes appeared to me in a different light: one was the scene where the Jewish barber soaps and shaves a customer's face to Brahms's *Hungarian Dance No.5*; and the other was the encounter between the two dictators Adenoid Hynkel / Adolf Hitler and Benzino Napaloni / Benito Mussolini, which ends in a screaming match.

They begin by looking at each other, but soon turn away, and finally each of them, wild-eyed, flings curses out into the world.

Incidentally, in Churchill's position I too would have been adamant that Sarah recited Schiller's "Bürgschaft" that evening. The ballad's last couplet is just too fitting:

Grant my request and let it be
Your band of two, henceforth be three!

30

The method of the clown. The attributes "queer and troubling and ghastly" used by William Knott to describe the "clown letter" are misleading. In truth the spiral of writing on the roll is evidence of a cool pragmatism. Churchill and Chaplin were pragmatists – more precisely, they were pragmatists capable of excitement. Those who claim that such an expression is an oxymoron are pragmatists incapable of excitement. The *method of the clown* is neither queer nor troubling, and nor is it ghastly – at least, not if it works, which means if it helps to drive away or at least reduce depression. And as they say: if it works, do it. Churchill got the method from Chaplin; Chaplin had it from Buster Keaton; and he had it from Harold Lloyd (as we know from a remark in Sylvia Davis's essay *Laughter without laughter. What's funny to Buster Keaton?* Los Angeles 1976, published privately to mark the tenth anniversary of BK's death; though the information is termed a "rumour" in: Marion Meade: *Buster Keaton: Cut to the Chase, a Biography.* New York 1995). Lloyd is supposed to have seen a workman repainting the face of the clock on a dizzyingly high church tower. The man got into difficulties, and because no one could hear his cries, he wrote "Help!" between the hands with his brush. He was clinging to the hand as he wrote, which turned under his weight so that the letters formed a semi-circle. From below, his limbs looked like the hands of the clock. Harold Lloyd, who suffered from terrible panic attacks, was greatly cheered by the spectacle. From it, he developed the "method of the clown" – the term was his – and passed it on to friends who were fellow sufferers. The experience also fed into the most famous scene in his film *Safety Last!* in which he dangles from the hand of a clock high up on a building. Lloyd told his colleague

Buster Keaton that a few experiments in which he lay on a sheet
of paper, writing a letter to himself in a spiral, had cured him of
his affliction; he also believed that the journeyman painter up on
the clock tower had really been an angel. He was sure that was so,
replied the staunch atheist Keaton, and he asked Lloyd to describe
the "method" to him in detail.

The first written reference to the "method of the clown" appears
in Theodor W. Adorno's essay "A Framework for a Theory of the
Comic". It makes no reference to Buster Keaton, Harold Lloyd or
Chaplin, as we might expect, though it does mention the comedian W.C. Fields. As early as 1933, Adorno had marshalled some
thoughts on the subject for a lecture he was due to give to a Social
Democrat association at Cologne University. The Nazis banned the
society, and the lecture never took place. Soon afterwards, Adorno
emigrated to England and expanded his thoughts on the phenomenon of the comic in his little study in Oxford, as a side-line, so
to speak, and without letting anyone in on his thoughts. He did
eventually give a lecture on his preliminary conclusions, aboard the
ship that took him and his wife from London to New York in February 1938. In this lecture, he used the expression "method of the
clown" for the first time. He was describing a "potential approach
to the fear of the world's shamelessness." However, he didn't explain
where he had got the term, meaning that the people present – all
of them German emigrants – must have thought he'd invented it;
that it had suggested itself, so to speak. Among the listeners was
Reinhard Mangold, a nineteen-year-old "student" of Adorno's.
As a schoolboy, he had fled Frankfurt with his parents, and had
attended Adorno's "lectures" in Oxford; now he was travelling on to
America. (I use inverted commas here because Adorno was admitted to Merton College as an "advanced student". He had been a
lecturer in Germany, but hadn't received an official teaching permit
in Oxford; he gave lectures all the same.) Reinhard Mangold would

give himself a new name in the New World, and would be remembered as one of the most innovative and courageous film producers in the history of Hollywood. In 1965, not guessing that Adorno had lost the papers for his lecture, he told the story of his encounter with the philosopher and his ideas on comedy on a German television documentary about his life. He said he had been greatly inspired by these ideas, and recognised that their origins lay in the classic slapstick films, especially in the films of Charlie Chaplin. He proudly held his lecture notes up to the camera. Adorno happened to watch the documentary, and made contact with his former student via the production company. His student sent him his notes by return of post. The philosopher used them to reconstruct his old thoughts, and filled them out with new thoughts – though, remarkably, there were still no reflections on the art of Charlie Chaplin (about whom he had already written two essays, published in the collection *Ohne Leitbild: Parva Aesthetica*). From this, he built his "Framework for a Theory of the Comic", at the centre of which is the *method of the clown*. He never managed to finish the essay, which means we still aren't told how the term reached Adorno – if indeed he ever intended to enlighten us on the matter. I should like to give a brief summary here of what Adorno says on the *method of the clown*.

The comic – he explains – is "an un/kind offering to *schadenfreude*". And *schadenfreude* is a form of cruelty. To laugh means to laugh *at* somebody, and as such it is a form of punishment, visited by a crowd upon an individual who has unconsciously transgressed their norms, to make him aware of his transgression. Here, Adorno is following the French philosopher Henri Bergson's thoughts, as laid out in his work on laughter, *Le rire. Essai sur la signification du comique*, in the year 1900. One of Bergson's theories may be summarised as: in order for the individual and the community to survive, the individual must keep to the generally observed mores. Serious transgressions will land him in court; minor ones are sanctioned in other ways – for example, being laughed at. If a man

–unintentionally – slips on a banana skin, we punish him with our *schadenfreude*, because slipping on a banana skin can be dangerous: next time he should pay more attention! Adorno's new thought is that comedy is a *conscious*, *intentional* offering to *schadenfreude*. He explains this with reference to the work of W.C. Fields.

Fields's comedy is based on breaking taboos. When he says – his most famous *bon mot* – that anyone who hates small dogs and children can't be all bad, we laugh because it is extremely reprehensible to hate small dogs and children, and we affirm our loathing of such people if – following Aristotle's theory of catharsis – for the short duration of our laughter we pretend to be just that kind of swine who does hate them. And we laugh in the awareness that W.C. Fields thinks just as we do, and that his joke is intended to affirm the rightness of his opinion and our own. So Fields breaks a taboo, and thereby illustrates the necessity of the taboo – namely, that we mustn't hate small dogs and children. But that isn't what W.C. Fields's comedy is about. His intention isn't to tell a joke. He actually does hate small dogs and children. And when he says that Felix Hoffmann is a better Messiah than Jesus, because the latter turned water into wine, but the former turned poppies into heroin, which makes people far happier, that is not intended as a joke, either. W.C. Fields didn't tell jokes. He never described himself as a comedian; he was a juggler, he said – which everyone took to be a joke. He seduces us into being just as wicked as he is. And even if we pretend not to notice, if we pretend that this fat man with his bad manners and his drug and alcohol problem is a plain old "good" taboo-breaker, who isn't actually breaking any taboos – we know, we know very well that he isn't funny, he's evil. So why do we laugh? Bergson, Adorno and many others before them who wrestled with the problem of comedy unanimously agree that comedy lies in the height from which you fall. If the pope passes wind, it's funnier than if Mr Smith lets one go. When Chaplin dines on his shoe, as if it were a delicacy from an upmarket Paris restaurant, it makes us laugh because it's a shoe and nothing more, and a filthy one at that. And it makes us laugh when W.C. Fields confides in us – puny, ridiculous little philistines that we are – that he does something as wicked as hating small dogs and children. Or setting up concentration camps. We ourselves would never dare to do that! Adorno thinks that Fields succeeds in exposing a bourgeois hatred of everything pure and beautiful, a hatred buried deep within us, which leads to an inferiority that we feel at all times. We split ourselves in two, we see ourselves both dwarfish and monstrous – and find both of these funny. We find *ourselves* funny. And there you go: for a little while, the world can't hurt us.

So the *method of the clown* consists of nothing more than making a person seem ridiculous to himself – with the aim of making him feel alienated from himself. All alone, it's impossible for a person to laugh at himself, because laughter always means laughter at someone else's expense. He has to split himself into a self that laughs, and another that is laughed at. That's the aim of the method.

From Adorno's biography we know that he was occasionally haunted by the black dog. His essay doesn't mention the practical application of the *method of the clown* – lying face-down on a sheet of paper, turning like the hand of a clock and writing a letter to oneself in a spiral. He was ashamed. At some point, so people say, his housekeeper caught him doing it.

PART FOUR

31

In May 1939 Chaplin received a phone call from a woman who introduced herself as "Hannelore" and spoke with a pronounced, German-sounding accent (Chaplin failed to specify later whether it really was a German accent, or if he just thought it was). She said she wanted to meet him – it was purely in his own interest, not hers. Normally Chaplin managed to deflect these approaches. Normally he didn't even answer the phone: at the studio, he left it to the telephonist, Miss Nicolaisen, or his secretary, Mrs Pryor, and at home he let Kono Toraichi decide whether a call should be put through to him or not. Women – it was always women – somehow got hold of his number on a regular basis, and he had already changed all his phone numbers twice, which involved a lot of tiresome bureaucracy.

He was on his own in the house. The chauffeur had taken Paulette and the children, Charles Jr. and Sydney, to the Griffith Park Zoo to see the Siberian tiger which was on loan from San Diego Zoo for a year. And, probably coincidentally, his staff all had the afternoon off or were running errands. He didn't know why everyone was out at the same time. Half an hour previously the house had been filled with noise, like it always was when the children – who wouldn't be children for much longer – were visiting their father: laughter, games, horseplay, the table piled far too high with nothing but their favourite foods, so Lita would have no excuse to complain to the child welfare service. Then suddenly, there was silence. Everyone had gone out – coincidentally or not – and he was alone. The telephone rang. And although he couldn't really tell, because he had no ear for the German language, he *thought* he could hear that the accent was put on.

The woman gave him the name of a bistro in Westwood. She would be there in an hour, and she'd wait for him; they only spoke French there. What did she mean by that, he tried to ask, but she had already hung up.

He didn't tell anyone where he was going. He could have called a friend, or his brother. He could have left a note on the hall table. It would have been the responsible thing to do. There had been an incident six months before, while he, Paulette and a few friends were staying near Carmel. They had gone on an excursion to Point Lobos, to admire the wild Californian coastline. There had been ten of them. They took three cars. They parked near the cliffs, looked down at the choppy waters of the Pacific Ocean and drank champagne. Suddenly a man stepped out of the bushes – a madman, as the police later tried to reassure them. He bowed to Paulette with the words, "Please, Miss Goddard, step aside," greeted Dan James and Tim Durant, who were standing next to Paulette, with smiles and nods, then pulled a small dagger from the inside pocket of his trench coat and strode towards Chaplin with a stiff-legged gait, the weapon in his outstretched arm, pale and dark at once, a picture-book bogeyman. Everyone froze – apart from Durant, who twisted the man's arm out of its socket, threw him to the ground, put his boot on his neck and pressed his head into the sandy soil. The man didn't put up any resistance. He allowed himself to be tied up with his own belt and those of the men present, and even helped them do it, smiling though his face was racked with pain, and nodding again, this time through tears, to Paulette. Then Durant, James and the other men – with the exception of Chaplin – bundled him into a car and laid him face-down on the back seat. Fat David Saddik sat on him, bending his arm upwards and holding it tight, like a lever for causing pain. One of Durant's friends transported them into town; the others followed. They handed the man over to the sheriff – amid much laughter. Chaplin asked the police officers to handle the matter discreetly, and not to pass anything on to the press. He was afraid another, less friendly madman might get the same idea and carry it out in a less amateurish fashion. He took it for granted that his friends would keep quiet about the incident. But the day after next, the *Los Angeles Daily News* led with the story that Mr Charles Chaplin had narrowly escaped an assassination attempt. The paper even knew the culprit's motives (plural!). There were certain groups, it said, who had taken against the fact that Chaplin was planning to make a movie ridiculing the German Chancellor Adolf Hitler. Chaplin was put through to the paper's editor-in-chief and bawled him out over the phone; how had he come by this absurd claim? Mr Wilson replied that a serious journalist never revealed his sources, and hung up. At that point, Chaplin had in fact begun preparations for the film he would eventually call *The Great Dictator*. He had personally shaken the hand of everyone involved in the project before they started work, looked into their eyes and ordered them not to breathe a word about it, to anyone at all, not their husband, their wife, their lover, their best friend. One of them must have talked. From then on, the studio was besieged by reporters, and finally Chaplin put out a press release in which he informed people that he was "entertaining the idea of producing a film about the current political situation in Europe, particularly in Germany" – Hitler and the Nazis. He didn't mention that he was intending to speak out against their barbarism. In the *New York Times*, however, the film critic Louella Parsons still announced, without a question mark: "Chaplin's next film is a burlesque on Hitler!" The *Denver Post* and the *Detroit Times* said something similar. The German consul, Dr Georg Gyssling, sent a letter of protest to the president of the United States, intimating that such a film would sorely damage the good relations between the German Reich and the USA. William Dudley Pelley, the leader of the Silver Shirt Union, the American equivalent of the Nazis' paramilitary *Sturmabteilung*, wrote an article attempting to stir up hatred against Hollywood's Jews, and repeating claims from the *Stürmer* and other Nazi newspapers that Chaplin was a Jew whose real name was Karl Thronstein. Jesse Maugh, one of the porters at the Chaplin Studio, stood speechless at the gates one morning: somebody had emptied a load of slurry outside. There was a letter from an anonymous reader in the *Chicago Tribune,* which said that if Chaplin really did try playing his dirty Jewish games with the highest representative of the German Reich, it would be "his own personal downfall". Friends urged Chaplin to press charges against the newspaper for printing this filth; the writer was obviously making a play on one of Hitler's speeches, where he spoke of the "downfall of the Jewish race", meaning its extermination. Chaplin declined. "This is America," he said. "America is a free, democratic country. People are free to say what they like here, and other people are free to ignore it." All the same, the Los Angeles Police Department put Chaplin under protection. Two plain-clothes officers followed him wherever he went. When he was at home, they sat in their Ford 35 at the bottom of Summit Drive, smoking and watching the villa's driveway – and being watched themselves, by nosy parkers and tourists. Only when Chaplin threatened to take them to court were the officers stood down.

His friends were surprised. "Aren't you afraid?" asked Dan James, who was helping with the screenplay.

"No," Chaplin replied. And he was surprised at himself – surprised that working on material that was closer to reality than any of his previous pictures could lift him so far away from this reality. He felt like he was living in a fairy tale.

He called a taxi – not a car from GY Taxi Service as usual, but from another company he'd never used before; he didn't give his name. He was phoning from a call box, he said – without having been asked – and he'd be waiting on the street. He put on light, loose clothes, a hat and sunglasses, went out to the street and stood a few paces down from the driveway. He had "such a feeling" – a feeling of adventure – but perhaps, he admitted in hindsight, he was reading more into it than there had actually been at the time. Perhaps he had just been curious.

He was not satisfied with his life.

Which didn't mean he was dissatisfied with himself; he certainly wasn't starting to doubt himself or suffering from the familiar, dreaded visions of failure and capitulation – no, he was dissatisfied because he thought himself capable of more than being funny and producing comic films. He felt he had something else to give. Not something greater – when he had finished this film, people would see that few things were greater – something different. He wanted to write a work on economics. He had a notebook full of ideas. He had been interested in issues of economics and equity for a long time. His work on *Modern Times* had been the fruits of his interest, not the catalyst for it, and at first, the fact that the Tramp infuriated both capitalists and communists had been a bitter pill to him. But he had united these irreconcilable camps in their outrage at the very appearance of this man on film – the weakest, the quietest, the most deserving of sympathy. And for him, that pointed to the possibility that the *method of the clown* could also heal the soul of society.

He had shown the world the twisted nature of an economy that makes humans into the slaves of machines; the Tramp had countered the madness with madness, he had twisted the view of reality by those few degrees necessary to show reality exactly as it was. During his visit to Berlin, which was now over ten years ago, he had discussed economics with Albert Einstein, including the fascinating and simple programme of a man called Silvio Gesell, who was against ground rent and interest, because these had an inherent tendency to redistribute wealth from the bottom to the top, and thus to perpetuate injustice and make the world ever more ugly. (He hadn't read anything by Gesell, but he had listened very closely as the people he usually listened to, Herbert Oakley and Ben Eichengreen, one an anarchist, the other a Marxist, talked about his theories.) Einstein had given him the book he had just finished reading: *The Theory of Economic Development* by Joseph Schumpeter (a German edition, unfortunately), and had written a dedication in it: "For Charlie Chaplin, the economist". That gave him something to think about. He wrote a short story. The first he had ever written. He felt like a young poet, like Keats must have felt, or Shelley, their genius sensing that they didn't have much time left. As he closed his hand around the fountain pen, he felt his heartbeat in his fingers. The story was called "Rhythm". In April of the same year it was translated and published in the French magazine *Cinemond*. It was set in the Spanish civil war. A man is to be executed. The officer in charge of the firing squad is a friend of the condemned man; until the very last he hopes for news of a reprieve. Finally he has no choice: he has to give the order, which consists of four rhythmical instructions: "Attention! ... Shoulder arms! ... Present arms!... Fire!" Just before the last word, he hears footsteps: it's the messenger who will save his friend. He shouts: "Stop!" Too late. Following habit – following the rhythm – the soldiers fire. A literary critic (one of the most respected critics, as Chaplin later heard, though he couldn't remember the name) described the story as a masterpiece, worthy of being mentioned in the same breath as the best. That gave him something to think about. Genius, he thought he remembered reading in something by Edgar Allen Poe, revealed itself in everything: if a poetic genius turned his attention to music, he would also be a musical genius; a musical genius would become an artistic genius, an artistic genius would become a political genius, et cetera. That also gave him something to think about. He was certain he possessed genius, and he was moved and humbled by this fact. The high knocking in his breast that heralded something new, big, different, made him glad and curious – and dissatisfied. Putting together the script for this film about the dicta-tor of a fictitious country had taken more energy than any material he had developed before, but the effort had not been painful. He knew it would be his greatest film; it would be the greatest work of cinematic art there had ever been. When this film was finished, he wouldn't make another for a long time – maybe never again. He would start a new life in a new art form – or become an academic, or a politician, a rhetorician, a tribune, a Demosthenes, a Cicero, a Dante.

He was not satisfied. In an expectant way, like a man about to marry, he was not satisfied. Maybe the phone call was the first push towards this new, great, different future – and maybe later he would say: it all started with a phone call in May 1939...

He was right.

32

It was unlikely that anyone recognised him. Nothing about his head looked like the Tramp. His hair was white, and without make-up his cheeks were starting to look a little slack. The sunglasses didn't suggest the wearer was trying to hide behind them; May afternoons in Los Angeles were very bright. And most men wore hats. In any case, he had discovered that people are easier to recognise by the way they move than by their faces. Nothing about his gait looked like the Tramp. When he entered the bistro on Wilshire Boulevard, he pursed his lips slightly, as the Tramp had never done, and mimicked the gait of Douglas Fairbanks, as he had got into the habit of doing recently, both consciously and unconsciously – he missed Doug. He hadn't seen him since his divorce three years previously. He no longer lived at Pickfair, and people said he wasn't doing too well, that all he did these days was drink. Mary had stopped coming to visit as well. Everything had changed. He kept meaning to invite Doug over for an afternoon of tennis.

The bistro was dimly lit, and he couldn't see anything. He took off the sunglasses. The L-shaped bar left just enough room to squeeze past the bar stools. Two men were standing together, talking to the bartender. They glanced at him, without interest, and went on talking. He took a seat at the bar, as far away from them as possible. The bartender walked over slowly, wiping the brass plate with his cloth as he went, and asked what he could get him, in English with a broad Californian accent – so much for only French being spoken here. He ordered a white wine. The bartender slid the customary glass of water over to him. It smelled of chlorine. Some people didn't like the smell, but he did, though he'd never seen anyone actually drink it. Could he have a sandwich with his wine? Yes he could. Swiss cheese? Swiss cheese.

He waited. Ate his sandwich, drank his wine. Smelled the chlorine. One of the men said goodbye, and nodded to Chaplin as well. Not because he had recognised him. Because he had manners. The other flicked through the sports pages of the newspaper, the cigarette jutting from his lower jaw at a sharp angle, then he said goodbye and left as well. The bartender could read the signs; the fact that this customer had taken a seat so far back meant he didn't want to talk. Now and then he glanced over, in case the customer wanted anything.

Chaplin waited. Waited for three quarters of an hour.

A man and a woman came into the bar. She was tall, brunette and very slender; she had put up her hair in a French roll, her face shimmered white, and she was wearing a dusky pink dress and a broad white belt with a three-pin buckle. The two of them walked over to him. The man gave him a friendly smile, held out his hand – without introducing himself – and said that unfortunately Hannelore had an urgent appointment, and she had to leave. Her lips and fingernails were the same shade of red. Avoiding his eye, she turned and left the bistro, without having said anything, without having shaken his hand. The man watched her go until she had vanished in the shimmer of the street. He said he was afraid he couldn't stay for long, either. He was wearing a light suit with a hint of pink in it and a Stetson of the same colour, with a deep blue band. His tie was deep blue as well. His right ring finger boasted a gold ring set with an oval onyx stone. His sunglasses were pale-coloured, light enough to see the room, but dark enough to hide the characteristics of his eyes.

The man ordered an Apollinaris. Once the bartender had moved away, he said that if Chaplin didn't take care, he would be dead in a year at most. He mustn't interrupt – as he had mentioned, he didn't have much time. He just had to listen. If Chaplin didn't take care, he would commit suicide in a year at most; he would believe it was his own decision, but in truth, without realising, he would be driven to it. He had to be aware that he was dealing with people who had mastered the most subtle methods of warfare. Eliminating him was an act of warfare. That was all he had to say. He meant well. He said Chaplin could have the mineral water.

With that, the man turned and was gone. Maybe he heard the question at his back: "But why?" But probably not. It had been spoken very quietly.

Chaplin asked the bartender for a pencil and paper, and wrote down what the man had said. He could remember every word. He described the woman's appearance, her face, her clothes, the way she walked; he did the same for the man. He described the sound of his voice: neither particularly soft, nor particularly penetrating, nor was there any discernible accent; what had struck him was the inappropriately matter-of-fact tone.

He asked the bartender for another sheet of paper. Described the woman's scent, which most likely came from her perfume, but awoke in him the memory of leather; she had smelled of leather, a sharp background note of leather. He didn't believe she was Hannelore. She hadn't spoken because she wasn't German and couldn't put on a German accent and had a completely different voice. There had been fear in Hannelore's voice, he thought he remembered – and he wrote that down as well – the kind of fear that shoots through you when you've done something momentous from which there is no way back, something that will bring about your own annihilation. She had spoken no more than four or five sentences on the phone, and from the first to the second and the third the fear had crept into her voice and gradually taken possession of it, first suppressing her initial assertiveness and then changing it into a childish, pleading anxiety; the final words had been spoken tremulously, and in the end she had been close to tears. He had been spellbound by this emotional rollercoaster, which had spanned so few syllables – that was the only reason, if he was honest with himself, that he had agreed to meet her in the bistro on Wilshire Boulevard. Had

Hannelore been coerced – forced, even – to speak to him on the phone? Was somebody hiding behind her voice? Was the German accent, or the imitation of a German accent, an intentional signal? Was it supposed to hint at which way the wind was blowing? Did somebody believe the conversation would be recorded and analysed afterwards? Had they taken that into account? It was well known that the industrialist Francis W. Purkey had his phone tapped to record all his calls: it was a machine that might have come from a utopian film, which took up a large table in Purkey's office and came on automatically as soon as the telephone rang. Purkey had bought it when one of his children was kidnapped. Chaplin had a wooden model of the machine made for *Modern Times*, but then decided not to place it in the office of the steel company's boss, out of respect.

He wrote everything down: his memories, his observations, his thoughts, his associations, his speculations. He wrote and wrote and wrote. He wrote for an hour, ordering a second glass of white wine, and then a third. Without being asked, the bartender handed him another sheet of paper.

He asked the bartender if he knew the man and the woman, or had at least seen them before. He hadn't. He asked what the two of them had looked like in his memory, which was an hour old. The bartender gave a brief description that tallied with his own. He added the observation that the man stooped a little; he had a slight suggestion of a hunchback. He'd noticed that as the man left the bar. The bartender didn't ask why his customer wanted to know all this. Hollywood was too close by for that. Bartenders in this neighbourhood weren't surprised by anything. The stoic, tired eyelids told him that, and he knew very well it would be understood. And it was understood. Chaplin noted down this observation, too.

On his way home in the taxi, he had a pleasant sense of fulfilment. The knowledge that such a feeling wasn't appropriate when he had just been informed of his impending death – death by his own hand, at that – couldn't drive it away.

33

During their first meeting in Los Angeles, Churchill and Chaplin had agreed to develop a story for a picture together – a picture about Napoleon. On the thorny descent through Carbon Canyon, with torn trouser legs below them, and above them the world's white hot umbilical cord, they batted one scene after another back and forth between them. The hero should be the Emperor's doppelganger. He turns up in Paris when the real Napoleon is far away in St Helena. He is admired and celebrated, and the people want to see him back on the throne. He doesn't know what he's doing; he tries to explain who he really is. Nobody listens to him. In the end, *he* doesn't know who he is any more either. He takes his own life. There is an official period of state mourning. By this point the real Napoleon has managed to escape. He returns to France. But the people point and laugh at him, as if he were the Emperor's monkey. He orders the people who mock him to be executed. Then they just laugh at him all the more. When nobody believes in him, he loses all power. He ends up as a *clochard*, playing the great Napoleon for the amusement of his homeless comrades under the bridges of Paris.

Nothing came of the project. But Chaplin was still preoccupied with the motif of the doppelganger. The idea of playing two roles at once in a film held a hypnotic attraction for him. The catalyst for his first thoughts about *The Great Dictator*, in which he finally used this motif, had been less his political concerns than the aesthetic challenge of playing against himself: using the old craft of pantomime *and* the first words he would ever speak on film, "to let the one annihilate the other". Roland Totheroh, his faithful cameraman, who had worked on every film since the start of the United Artists era, said afterwards that nobody had talked about politics during the filming. "If Charlie had looked like Stalin," he said, to disillusion people who regarded the Chaplin of this period as a political artist first and foremost, "the film would have gone up against Communism. If he'd looked like the pope, it would have become a campaign against Catholicism. But he happened to look like Hitler."

Did he really look like him?

Everyone always makes reference to their little moustaches, particularly in caricatures. But apart from that? If we look at photos from the period, random street scenes, whether in Germany, Australia or America, we will notice that the men are wearing hats, most of them bowlers (like the Tramp), and a lot of them have that ominous toothbrush moustache – more often a rectangle like Hitler's; less often a trapezium like the Tramp's. The intense discussion that took place about whether Hitler had copied this emblem from the once-admired clown then appears absurd – millions of other men would have to be subject to the same suspicion. All the more surprising, then, that long before Chaplin himself decided to play the German dictator, the public had come up with the idea themselves.

There are two incidents I would like to mention.

The first story comes from Charlie Chaplin Jr. In his memoirs of his father (I own only the German edition: *Mein Vater Charlie Chaplin*, Diana Verlag, Konstanz 1961) he writes that in the mid-thirties, his father was sent an article from a French newspaper, with a translation enclosed, which said that Hitler had banned Chaplin films in Germany. And why? Because in the opinion of leading German physiognomists, the Tramp bore too much resemblance to the Führer. (Actually – and this is my own research – the German *Sixth Provision on the Implementation of the Moving Picture Law* of 3 July 1935 contains a paragraph on Charlie Chaplin, with the customary reference to his supposed Jewishness and the statement that henceforth his films may not be shown in German cinemas.)

The French paper, I have also discovered, was the *Paris-Midi*; it featured a bold headline: "In his next film, Chaplin will appear without his legendary moustache, so that he is not mistaken for Hitler." The story that follows is both entirely fabricated and clairvoyant. How the author – one Gaston Thierry – happened upon it, nobody knows. Chaplin later tried several times to get in touch with him, but to no avail. Charlie Chaplin, Thierry wrote, was currently – this was 1935! – working on an anti-Hitler propaganda film. It contained the following central scenes: the Tramp, with his little moustache as usual, enters a barber shop. He looks at pictures of famous personalities. "He stops in front of Hitler's picture. He touches his own moustache. Filled with a sudden rage, he snatches up a razor, shaves it off with a single stroke...and leaves again". And Thierry assures readers: "Chaplin plays the scene with such expression that the meaning of the gesture cannot be misunderstood." He claims to have it on good authority that "even though the film may well be banned in Germany, incurring significant financial losses for Chaplin, he refuses to cut the scene at any cost". Not a word of it true!

The whole thing is uncanny. And Chaplin found it uncanny, too. In 1935 he had not even considered making a film anything like this. But – his son remembers – from then on "the idea began to take shape within him". Chaplin also tried to find out who had sent him the article, together with the English translation – but to no avail. Forty years on, thinking about it still made him feel queasy. He told Josef Melzer that in hindsight he felt like Macbeth: the witches had prophesied what would become of him, and he then put all his effort into becoming that very thing. Chaplin had put all his effort into transforming Gaston Thierry's brazen lies into reality.

The second incident took place the following year. The idea of playing Hitler had taken hold in Chaplin, "it was multiplying within me". He was spending most of his time outside Hollywood, avoiding his usual circle of friends – "the same voices, the same thoughts". He wanted unfamiliar voices and unfamiliar thoughts. And he found them, as I have said, in Carmel-by-the-Sea, south of San Francisco. One of his new friends – he couldn't remember who it was – suggested giving Hitler a twin brother, a layabout, whom the Führer locked up in a concentration camp as soon as he came to power, to get him out of the way. And this twin brother, the Tramp, who else – this was the plot they sketched out during a jolly evening together – gets taken along when the prisoners stage a breakout. They hide in a laundry room overnight, find SS uniforms there, change their clothes and march through the twilit city, where the Tramp is taken for the Führer. The people cheer him and carry him to the Reich Chancellery on their shoulders. When the real Führer gets back from his holiday, everyone laughs at him, and eventually they put him away in a madhouse. The way he talks seems mad to them – although it's no different to what he was saying before. Chaplin improvised scenes all evening. There was a lot of laughter. He woke up in the night, certain in the knowledge that this wasn't it. In the morning, he decided to seek out different friends once more. He went to stay with Ben and Ethel Eichengreen, both fervent Marxists and members of the Communist Party.

I should place a large question mark over the following story; it is fed by only one source, and, as I have mentioned, most exegetes of Chaplin's work and life regard this source as dubious: I am referring to the *Interview With the Tramp* by Erica Southern, alias Lilian Bosshart.

One evening Chaplin was at Ben and Ethel Eichengreen's, in their quaint, book-lined little house between Carmel and Monterey. While the two of them prepared dinner, he walked down to the shore in the last of the light, where there was a group of redwoods – "the watchmen at the end of the West," as Ethel called them. And there he saw a figure walking along the waterline, a long way off, dressed in black – a long coat, a hat. It was a man, a rabbi who looked like he'd come from the film *Die Stadt ohne Juden*; he walked towards him across the pebbly beach, spread his arms wide and called out: "Mr Chaplin, Mr Chaplin, what luck, meeting you here! They say you come here every evening to bid the sun goodnight. I've been waiting for you." He had a long, dark beard, ear-locks, and glasses with thick lenses, his eyes unreal behind them. He grasped Chaplin's hands and kissed them and said: "I thank you, Mr Chaplin, and all my friends thank you as well, for making a film about that fiend, and showing him to the world as he really is: evil." Chaplin asked how the man knew he wanted to make such a film. Everyone knew, the man replied, every decent person in the world. And there was something else everyone knew: he would be wonderful as a Jew who vanquished the great enemy, the evil Haman. "So I'm going to play a Jew, am I? Well, I didn't know that," he said. "But of course you do, of course you know that!" the man cried out. "What sort of Jew will I play then?" "A little man, a simple man, a weak man, the weakest of them all." "And he will vanquish the fiend?" "Because in his heart he is a Golem." And then the man walked back down to the water's edge. His nephew was waiting, he called out, and he couldn't keep him waiting any longer. But there was nobody there. The sun had gone down, and Chaplin was standing under the gigantic trees. He expected to wake up. But he hadn't been dreaming. He walked back to Ben and Ethel's low, thatched house. Up on the coast road, the cold evening air made him quicken his pace. And again he had the feeling that he must put all his effort into transforming a prophecy into the truth – the prophecy of a rabbi on the shore of the Pacific Ocean. He told his friends about the encounter, and Ben said it was a serviceable idea for a story. "That business with Hitler's twin brother was always nonsense!" And Ethel agreed with her husband: "The Tramp is a Jew, that's what everyone thinks anyway. Play Hitler, *and* a Jew who looks like Hitler! It'll be a hoot!"

From that moment on, he worked on the story as we know it,

first as a hazy notion, then as an idea, and later as the script he wrote with Dan James (he took particular delight in this work; the young, gifted James managed to awaken in him a desire to write dialogue, and he had already been prepared to throw out all his theories about silent film). Then he worked on it behind the camera and in front of the camera, with the largest team he would ever command. And finally he worked on it by day with Willard Nico at the cutting table, and by night with the composer Meredith Willson at the cello and piano. He was possessed by this work. As Charlie Chaplin Jr. tells us: the film was both a blessing and a heavy burden for his father. It was all so easy for him, and so hard at the same time. Day after day, he looked forward to nothing more than the work, but also to nothing more than finally, finally being finished with it. "What must be must be," he said every morning and every evening. When Charlie Jr. once asked him what he meant by that, his gruff reply to the twelve-year-old was that he didn't know himself; something in his head was speaking this sentence to him, some days a hundred times, others a thousand times.

Charlie, doubled – that was the fundamental stroke of genius behind the film: Charlie as a ludicrous dictator *and* as a Jewish barber. That was a slap in the face for the fiend. Only one other person hit him as hard: Winston Churchill – though he didn't use the weapons of the clown.

34

Then Kono resigned.

One morning there was an envelope on Chaplin's breakfast plate. It contained a card with a hand-written message on it:

Dear Mr Chaplin,
I request release from your service, and your friendship.
Kono Toraichi

It was half past four. At this hour, everyone in the house was usually asleep: Paulette and her maid, the cook, the butler, Frank Kawa and Kono. Chaplin would breakfast alone, noting down the day's agenda on a sheet of paper. Filming was to begin in a month's time. At six, Kawa and Kono would fetch him from the kitchen. This time Kawa came alone.

At first, according to Chaplin's son Charlie Jr., his father took the letter for a joke. His first thought was that somebody had crept into the house overnight and laid the card on his plate. His second thought was that Kono had learned how to be funny. *This message is real* was only his third thought. Kono was humourless. It was a characteristic that Chaplin particularly valued in his major-domo. Kono never laughed. Even when he laughed, he never laughed. They never laughed when they were discussing a new gag. If the gag was good, Kono would say: "People will laugh." Nothing more was to be expected, not from Kono and not from the gag.

Kono had been in Chaplin's service for eighteen years. He was as much a part of his life as Syd was. The advantage of Kono over Syd was that Chaplin worried very often and very deeply about the latter's state of mind, but never about the former's. He knew nothing

about Kono's private life, if there even was such a thing. And he felt
no regret about that. And he knew – he thought he knew – that
Kono didn't expect it, either. Kono was married. When and where
and how this marriage had taken place, nobody could imagine.
Kono was always there. Sometimes Chaplin didn't need him, and
then he wasn't there. He had entered his service at the age of seven-
teen, as a chauffeur. A Japanese immigrant, he had learned English
in a remarkably short space of time, first fluently, then flawlessly,
and finally with absolute mastery, commanding an unparalleled
wealth of words and imagery. He had a Shakespeare quotation for
every trick life played on you; he could recite long passages from
Moby Dick and dictate letters in Chaplin's style. He was promoted
to private secretary, and nominated himself as a bodyguard. (On
certain occasions, about which his boss did not wish to be more
precisely informed, he carried a gun, and when asked whether
he would ever use it, he nodded, in his incomparably succinct
manner). Long afterwards, Chaplin would say in a radio interview:
"He was my Man Friday". He was ashamed of having said it – he
called the broadcaster and asked them to edit out the passage. The
producer promised, but didn't keep his word. Kono was also Chaplin's muse, "the only ideal muse", as he recalled. He listened without
speaking a word; nothing could be gleaned from his expression. He
was another very private private secretary. And he was his friend.
Or rather: he had been his friend for a single night – in May 1931,
in Juan-les-Pins, when the master looked after the servant, who had
been struck down with ptomaine poisoning. The master pressed
his servant's hands and turned his eyeballs upwards and prayed
aloud: "Let my friend live, please, please, let my friend live!" When
the servant woke from a long, deep sleep, and the worst was over, he
found the master still sitting at his bedside. He clutched his master's
hands and said it had been the word "friend" that had given him the
strength to survive. Later the two of them crafted a scene out of
this moment. For a talking picture. Some words do not diminish a

creation. Three pages of dialogue. They were waiting in the safe, to be used at some point.

Paulette liked Kono. But he didn't like her. He hadn't liked Lita, either. But she had given him good reason for that. She had slandered him, claiming he was a spy from a Japanese film company. She tried to ban Chaplin from discussing any ideas with Kono. "After all, any financial damage would affect me, too!" Paulette, by contrast, took every opportunity to say how much she valued Kono. And she meant it. She had never met a better organised person. It was just that she wanted to run the household herself. Kono seldom took an active role in managing the house, the kitchen, garden or garage, but whenever questions arose – whether the lobby should be repainted or modern steel pans bought, or a different company used to clean the carpets, or a new car or a new tennis net purchased – then he had the final say. But Paulette did what she did and didn't ask him. And for Kono, that was reason enough to resign.

His departure was as swift as his employment had been eighteen years before. Kono arrived and stayed. Kono left and was never seen again.

A week later, the shock woke Chaplin in the middle of the night.

He went into the kitchen and sat down on the floor by the range. His neck felt cold. He thought about Kono's reaction when he had told him about the phone call from "Hannelore". His face had been expressionless. During the long time they were together, Chaplin had never been able to read Kono's face the way he could with everyone else's. The art of reading faces made him superior to other humans. Had he not used his art with Kono? Or had he failed with him? Was it because this man's inner life meant nothing to him? He had looked into Kono's face after that phone call, and a thought had flared up in his mind: he knows. The thought was immediately extinguished again. And what if it was true? The resignation was absurd. Paulette wanted to speak to Kono; she was prepared to yield to him on everything. He declined. She thought her household management was just a pretext. And Chaplin thought it too. But what was behind the resignation?

If Kono had actually known in advance that "Hannelore" was going to call, then he probably also knew about the man and the woman from the bistro. Maybe he had chanced to hear somewhere, or someone had told him, that some kind of stupid prank was going to be played on Chaplin. One didn't need to consider the prankster's motive: madmen could knead water and fire into dough, and everyone knew there were plenty of madmen in this part of the world. So Kono hadn't taken the matter seriously, and hadn't wanted to trouble him with it, and now he was feeling guilty. So he resigned just because he felt guilty? Without any further explanation? After eighteen years? That was absurd! Or else it was something more than a joke. And Kono knew that, and knew even more. Knew who "Hannelore" was. Maybe the whole business was actually deadly serious. The man in the bistro had informed Chaplin that he would commit suicide before the year was out. There had been nothing of the prankster about him. Chaplin whisked two eggs in a shallow bowl, added a pinch of salt and a small cup of milk, and laid slices of white bread in the mixture. While they were soaking it up, he melted some butter in a pan. He loved French toast. He found the bottle of maple syrup in one of the cupboards. Seven years ago, when he had been in Japan with Sydney and Kono, there had been an incident that he wasn't really aware of at the time, though he'd been informed about it later – by the Los Angeles Police Department. Apparently a Japanese far-right organisation calling itself the Black Dragon Society had planned to assassinate him. A lieutenant from the Kwantung Army was arrested. Under interrogation he said that they had wanted to kill Charlie Chaplin because he was a famous personality and the darling of the capitalists; they thought his death might lead to a war with America. The LAPD officer had brought him this news, in a sepulchral voice, when he was safely back on American soil, and that evening he and his friends had laughed heartily about it. He had come up with a series of sketches on the theme, from which "the next best comedian would have made a film every year for the rest of his life" – as the producer Joseph Schenk said. Mrs Pryor wrote her fingers raw: the Tramp in Japan, waddling comically round the old temples, flirting with geishas, while bombs go off around him, daggers flash, pistols crack – he thinks the bombs are New Year's firecrackers, the daggers are a photographer's flash, and the bullets are annoying flies.

That had all been six years ago. Kono resigned three days ago. Without any reason he could understand. After all this time in his service.

35

The telephone in the lobby rang three times during the night. Paulette didn't hear it. But then Paulette wouldn't have heard the moon falling into the swimming pool. She took sleeping tablets and put wax in her ears. Although her bedroom *was* closer to the telephone than his, and the ringer was very loud – it was designed to be heard even if you were in the garden. Perhaps he'd just imagined it. Dreamed that "Hannelore" was calling him again. The staff wing was too far away, there was no point asking the maid or the cook or Frank Kawa. At the studio, he told Miss Nicolaisen to find out who the caller could have been. If anyone had called at all. "Hannelore's" voice had been close to tears by the time she had finished speaking, which led him to think she was under pressure, probably being forced to say what she said. Now he even thought he remembered her sounding as if she was reading lines. Someone had given her a script. Was she being used? And why her? Because of her German accent?

That afternoon, Miss Nicolaisen knocked on the door of the conference room where he was in discussion with Alf Reeves, Sydney, Dan James, the agent Toni G. Williams and the gentleman from the security firm, about the problems presented by the crowd scenes. And the costs. Syd thought he could save himself all this trouble and create a much more powerful effect using a sound collage from the Off. The boss could see the sense in that. Miss Nicolaisen beckoned him over. She whispered. Which she never usually did. She hadn't managed to find out who had called the previous night. But the phone had rung. Three times. Her friend at the phone company had confirmed it.

He ended the meeting. He had Frank Kawa drive him out to Pacific Palisades. He missed Kono. They would have walked along the beach together, and their conversation would have helped him work out what he would do next if he were the head of the Nazi commando that was targeting him. What if they'd persuaded Kono to join their side? In their position, that was what he'd do. He had always thought Kono the loyalest of the loyal. But anyone can be blackmailed. Kono had a wife. Our loved ones make hostages of us, in the clutches of the world. The Japanese far-right sympathised with the Nazis. If they really had set their sights on him, they would know everything about him. Know that his very private private secretary knew everything about him.

He told Kawa to collect all the newsreels, American, English, German, French, that showed Hitler – talking to children, cuddling babies, visiting the sick in the hospitals, inspecting military parades, posing between party comrades, giving speeches on every possible occasion, eating, picking his nose, belching – every photograph he could get his hands on, every recording, the English translation of *Mein Kampf*, everything. But he should bring them to Chaplin at home, not at the studio. Since Kono had gone, he had started entrusting Kawa with tasks that weren't actually part of his job, or commensurate with a chauffeur's salary. If Kawa demanded a rise, he would pass him on to Syd. Syd didn't care if people saw him as a miser.

It was a smart move, taking Kono away from him. He needed friends like he needed bread and water. If he were these people, he would slander him. There was no level of gaucherie or brutality he wouldn't stoop to. He would call him a money-grubbing Jew. A child molester. A talentless gurner. A thief, a liar, a semi-literate man feeding off the brains of others. At first, his friends would stand up for him. But if his attacker kept at it, took nothing back, qualified nothing, proved none of the accusations, made no arguments, just kept on insulting and smearing, disparaging and ridiculing, then his friends would grow quieter. Because they would see what would happen to them if they carried on backing him. Chaplin was the most famous, the most popular of them all. If there was no helping *him*, then who would help *them*? – so his friends would think. And they would pull away. And then they would start to think: really, a person can only come in for such crude, brutal treatment if there is something in the allegations. They had already taken Kono from him. Who would be next? They were clever. Clever madmen. If they simply shot him down or blew him up or stabbed him, like the Black Dragons had planned to do, they would create a hero, all-powerful, invincible. "The Nazis kill the most popular man in the world!" the headlines would read, on the front page of every newspaper in the world. No Nazi politician would be able to show his face anywhere – in the farthest reaches of Patagonia, people would point their fingers at him: "You murdered Chaplin!" He thought of the enthusiastic crowds who had greeted him in Berlin. It was hard to know who the Germans loved more: Adolf Hitler or Charlie Chaplin. The murderers' own people would turn against them. However, if it emerged that Charlie Chaplin had taken his own life while working on a film that would stir up hatred against the German Reich and its Chancellor, then a skilled propagandist like Mr Goebbels would have no trouble making his own people and the rest of the world believe that the little "fidgeting Jew", the "ghetto clown" from the depraved neighbourhood of Hollywood, had crossed over into the Promised Land out of guilt and shame.

Before they reached the Pacific Coast Highway, Chaplin hit on the idea of visiting Douglas Fairbanks in Santa Monica. Friends had told him that Doug was away most of the time, often in Europe: he'd bought a studio in Paris. He had married again. Would Doug be pleased to see his friend? Or by this point, had he already become a "former" friend? It was more than two years since he'd spoken to Mary, who still lived less than a hundred paces up the hill from him, in Pickfair, which now had a different name. Once they had waved to each other, when she was out watering her roses with a garden hose. He felt guilty about both of them. Not wanting to be dragged into the situation, to take Mary's side or Doug's, he had pulled away from both of them. He had never been to Doug's beach house in Santa Monica. He'd ignored the invitation to his housewarming. He hadn't sent a thank-you note, either. He'd left the card lying on his desk at home until the date of the party, and then torn it up and thrown it in the wastebasket.

It was just after two in the afternoon, and he found Doug drunk, but cheerful. Happy that his friend had come to visit.

"What do you know about my new project?"

The question shredded their laughter.

"Probably no more than everyone else in Hollywood," Doug replied, seriously.

"Do you know why I'm asking?"

"I believe so, yes."

"And why am I asking?"

"Don't come the inquisitor with me, Charlie," said Doug, laying a hand on his cheek. He did it in the way he always used to, and Chaplin had always loved it. "I'm not one of them. You must know that."

"One of whom?"

"Please, Charlie, say something without one of these question marks that are more like exclamation marks."

"They mean to finish me, Doug. I'm sorry if I sounded rude."

"It's their way of defending themselves, Charlie. And their way is not a subtle way. But that's all. Hitler can't order Roosevelt to stop you making a film about him."

"Do you think they know I'm visiting you?"

"Excuse me?"

"I believe they know about every step I take."

"Do you *believe* that Charlie, or do you *know* it?"

"What's the difference? I've started to believe it today. I feel it. That's like knowing it."

He told Doug about Kono Toraichi. Doug didn't seem surprised that he'd resigned. Why not? He had always got on well with Kono, as had Mary – more than once, and not entirely in fun, they had tried to lure him away to work for them. He'd left the decision up to Kono. The two of them would have paid him more. Kono hadn't even replied. Chaplin didn't touch the whisky Doug had poured him. He tried one of the chocolate biscuits. Why wasn't Doug surprised that Kono had gone? "Why are you here on your own?" he asked.

"Why do you think?"

"What should I do, Doug?"

"If you'd asked me that a year ago, I would have said: leave it be! Find another story. One that's better suited to Paulette."

"And why aren't you saying that now?"

"Because you're too far into the work. You've invested too much money. Too much effort. Too much passion. You can't stop now, but you don't want to go on."

"How do you know all that?"

36

Kawa did a good job. Without having been asked to, he got hold of a copy of Leni Riefensthal's documentary film about the 1934 Nuremberg Rally. Chaplin had already seen the film once. An agent – he couldn't remember his name now, one of these smarmy cynics who sold American films to Germany – had invited him to a showing in the screening rooms at Metro-Goldwyn-Mayer. Ten or so personalities from the industry were there, among them David Selznick and Irving Thalberg, the latter still fabulous, though already gravely ill. The agent gave a little speech, telling them how much Frau Riefenstahl admired the American film people and their business. One to one he was clearer: Frau Riefenstahl was especially keen for Chaplin to watch her film, and she would be delighted if he were to let her know what he thought. And with a wink, he added: even more delighted with an invitation to Hollywood. Chaplin had found the film laughable. A brilliantly staged, overblown piece of nonsense. (The Spanish director Luis Buñuel was also invited; he said in his memoirs: "Chaplin [...] laughed like a madman. And once so hard that he actually fell off his chair.") He had made a swift exit as the final credits were rolling. When the film was awarded a gold medal at the World Fair in Paris, and when further awards followed in France, Sweden, and even in the United States, he fell out with friends who accused him of not being able to differentiate between politics and art. Of course *Triumph of the Will* was propaganda for a loathsome ideology, they said, but at the same time it was the pinnacle of cinematic art, a better political film had never been made. The very essence of politics was that somebody was in favour of something while others were against it, but as an artist you had to rise above that, and judge a thing by purely aesthetic criteria. He had asked whether any of them would eat shit with this level of enthusiasm, if it had first been shaped and painted to look like a steak with Belgian fries and broccoli.

Now he was watching the film again, with Dan James. And enthusing about it. Frau Riefensthal was a great artist – and a captivatingly cunning comedian. She had provided him with the perfect reference material for Adenoid Hynkel. There were lengthy shots of Hitler. Every ridiculous detail of the dictator's gestures and speech patterns was captured on celluloid. He opened his mouth wide, barking the most banal nonsense out into the universe, and the camera was right there, probing this lipless scream-hole all the way to his tonsils, exploring his nostrils, exposing every bogey.

"If I were Hitler," he said to Dan James, "I'd wring Ms Riefen- stahl's neck."

Dan didn't find that funny.

"Order someone else to wring her neck."

Dan didn't find that funny either. Why not?

"As for me, I'd sue her," he said with feigned resignation.

But Dan didn't find that funny either.

Fine, Mr James could laugh at whatever he wanted to laugh at. It was a free country. And the screenplay was finished. He didn't need Mr James for the fine details. In any case, he was only going to write the big speech at the end – which he would give himself! – once the first edits were done. He still didn't know what he was going to say. There was still just a note in the treatment:

Charlie steps forward. He begins slowly – he is petrified. But his words give him strength. During the speech the clown is trans- formed into a prophet.

His idea was to give the speech from off screen. In shot: soldiers breaking out of their goose-step and into a waltz, or a firing squad laying down their guns, or troops starting to dance for joy during the speech. Or Paulette – Hannah's face, Hannah's eyes, sun beams breaking through clouds, cornfields and so on. Music: either something of his own or, in for a penny, Richard Wagner, in for a pound, the overture to *Lohengrin*. He didn't want the camera watching him as he spoke, at least, not if he was giving a longer speech, something with grammatical, syntactical and topical meaning – gibberish, on the other hand, was like pantomime: universally understood, a silent film with words. Nobody could help him with the closing speech. He announced there would be no further discussion about the crowd scenes. After Riefenstahl it was clear to him: he would show the crowds! He had to! No question about costs! The camera is positioned at Hynkel's back. We see the people he's speaking to – thousands of them. He told Syd to pay off Dan James and let him go.

Months after the fact, Chaplin heard on the grapevine that people in England were plotting against his film. How was it that the whole world knew what kind of film he was working on! After the prime minister, Neville Chamberlain, had signed the Munich Agreement in September of the previous year, the British political establishment was on edge, and embarrassingly anxious not to provoke Hitler, even if their concessions had only one purpose: feeding the beast in order to play for time. A member of parliament had written a letter to an undersecretary in the foreign office, expressing his "concerns" and calling on him to do everything in his power to make sure the film "in which Charles Chaplin intends to give a satirical portrayal of Mr Hitler" was banned in England. What was this man afraid of? That Hitler would bomb England because a film was shown there? In any case, the British film censors sent a telegram to the US censorship board asking for an explanation and the documents relating the project. They in turn contacted Chaplin's company, and received the response that none of these existed: there was no screenplay, no production schedule, no finance plan.

Chaplin couldn't discover who had given this response. On the one hand, he thought it was a pretty original answer; on the other, he was appalled that no one had informed him. He spent a whole morning yelling at everyone who crossed his path in the studio. In the afternoon he read an article in the *Hollywood Reporter,* which said Charlie Chaplin had realised it would "kick up a stink" if he attacked the elected head of a state that had good relations with the US government, and had therefore decided to give up on the project. The following day the papers were full of it, and the radio stations led with the story – ahead of the latest news on the war between China and Japan. The telephones rang off the hook, at home and in the studio. Once again, reporters gathered on Summit Drive. Reeves and Syd planted themselves in front of the boss, their legs forming a large M, and demanded an explanation – above all, an explanation of why he had spoken to one of these hacks before speaking to them. He hadn't, he shouted at them, he hadn't done anything of the sort. It was all lies! Invented by these very hacks! What had got into them, that they thought him capable of such a breach of trust! How was he supposed to work with people who saw him as some kind of underhand villain!

He put out a press release.

I wish to state that I have never wavered from my original determi-
nation to produce this picture. Any report, past, present or future to
the effect that I have given up the idea, is deliberately false. I am not
worried about intimidation, censorship or anything else.
(Signed: Charlie Chaplin)

It was his first public statement about *The Great Dictator.*

He was famous and popular. And he was famous and despised. Threatening letters arrived by the basketful. Most of the threats were directed towards "the Jew Chaplin". The Hays Office, the US film industry's censors, sent over a man who didn't let Chaplin get a word in edgeways – which was saying something! – and explained in the style and tone of a man collecting mafia protection money that United Artists could save themselves a whole heap of dough if they called a halt to all work on this picture immediately, because under no circumstances – he could promise them this without having seen so much as thirty feet of film – would they permit it to be shown in an American cinema. The same day the message arrived that the Chilean government had decided to ban Chaplin's latest film, in the belief that it was already finished. They heard similar things from Turkey and Japan and even France.

And finally the world also learned what the leader of the German Reich thought about all this: "The liberties taken by various organs whose mission is to poison the world's well can only be classed as an illegal crime." What might a *legal* crime look like, Sydney wondered.

A United Artists press office secretary and her boyfriend produced a catalogue of the insulting terms that German newspapers used to describe the boss: "Hanswurst stooge", "Archetypal Jew", "An actor aping psychopathic cretinism", "Hebrew libertine", "preposterous, glorified Galician nigger", "The clown of an inferior people", "a Jewish swine defiling the race", "a Bolshevist outside of office hours". And so on. The boyfriend came from a family of German-Jewish émigrés; he translated the expressions into English, she proudly presented the list to the boss, and the boss saw to it that she was fired within the hour.

Kawa wanted to prove he could do a good job, and he did too good a job. He answered the telephone and decided whether Mr Chaplin was available or not. When he heard a woman's voice with a German accent, he decided against her. And he didn't mention it to his boss. Since Kono had resigned, Kawa had started giving orders to all the staff he judged to be on his level or below. He too had watched *Triumph of the Will*. He only had a soft voice, but he could pull off the Führer's tone pretty well. And it proved effective.

He banned the maids from answering the phone. He also banned them from bothering Mr Chaplin. They should either let the phone ring or get Kawa, if he was there. One of the maids did allow herself to be intimidated by his tone, but only by his tone, and that didn't last long. She spoke to her boss, who was actually the only person she answered to. Asked disingenuously if what Mr Kawa had said was alright with him. It wasn't alright with him. He summoned Kawa and subjected him to an interrogation. Among the phone calls he had declined, had there been a woman with a German accent? Yes, there had. He must tell him word for word what she had said. Unfortunately, Kawa muttered, he hadn't waited to hear what she said – he had hung up. He begged the boss's forgiveness. But the boss didn't forgive him. He yelled at the chauffeur in the dictatorial voice he had recently mastered (him too!) and made Kawa repeat after him that he was just a chauffeur, and he only had that job for as long as Chaplin saw fit, and just then he didn't see fit, and he ordered Kawa to give him the keys for the Studebaker right that minute.

Chaplin drove to Carmel to see Ben and Ethel Eichengreen.

Forty years later, Dan James commented on Chaplin's behaviour at that time: "Of course he had in himself some of the qualities that Hitler had. He dominated his world. He created his world. And Chaplin's world was not a democracy, either. Charlie was the dictator of all those things."

37

The German Wehrmacht had invaded Poland. Chaplin heard the news on the radio in Ben and Ethel's kitchen. Ethel's mother came from Lublin, and had come to America with her parents when she was a child. Ethel sank onto the sofa and wept. This annoyed her husband. Since she'd gone through the change, he said, she cried at the drop of a hat. He poured her a glass of water. Couldn't he see, she wailed – and she drank, holding the glass with both hands – Hitler didn't care about Poland, why should he, there was nothing there, he wouldn't move into a country her grandparents had moved out of – it was about the Jews. Ha, Ben exclaimed, he liked that! She hadn't cried when Hitler marched into Czechoslovakia or when he marched into Austria. What was so special about the Jews to make her to cry over them? Weren't the Austrians people, too, and the Czechs? "I'm a Jew, and you're a Jew," said Ethel. "Everyone we know is Jewish, Herbert's a Jew, Charlie's a Jew. Hitler is marching against *us*!" Ben countered this with some kind of Marxist argument, and Hegel, and said anyway, Herbert Oakley was an anarchist, and an individual anarchist at that, so he was no use to anyone, he wasn't loyal to a race or a religion.

Chaplin couldn't listen. Not this time. He usually followed Ben's speeches with devotion, even delight; Ben had given him an introduction to historical materialism and political economics, and Chaplin had nodded until his neck ached as Ben explained the tendency of the rate of profit to fall, and the fetishistic nature of commodities. And he had listened spellbound when Ethel described the guys who went to the monthly meetings of the local branch of the Communist Party – obliging, sinister characters who she suspected retreated into Dostoyevsky's *Demons* at night and pulled the book cover closed behind them. But this time he heard his friends' voices as nothing more than music, and that was enough for him. With his back against the tiles of the clay stove that Ben and Ethel had built themselves (like everything else in the house), he stretched out his legs on the deep bench, and sat there like a doll. The heat made him tired and a little stupid. The two of them had always fought a running battle, but it was a battle of love between a couple wanting to keep their emotions in shape. He liked Ethel more than Ben, but only a little more. Ben was fat and his flesh sagged, while Ethel looked after herself. She kept her figure through exercise, ate plenty of vegetables, no meat, fish only if it was raw, and drank huge quantities of water. Her hair was grey, but with the vitality of a young girl's hair. They both painted – her paintings abstract, his figurative – and that was how they made their living.

For the first time, he told them about himself. And Ben and Ethel listened, as he had listened to them. He told them everything, right from the beginning, about the telephone call from the woman with the German accent who called herself "Hannelore"; about the man and the woman in the bistro on Wilshire Boulevard; about the night-time calls; about Kono and Kawa. He also told them that someone had predicted his suicide.

To his surprise they both agreed that he needed protection. Though professional protection, by a Hollywood security firm, was not a good idea, since the liberal press had recently discovered that over sixty per cent of these companies' employees described themselves as Nazi sympathisers, and more than a few were members of the Silver Shirts. Protection could only be guaranteed by people who shared his convictions. Without beating about the bush, there were only two organisations that could make such a guarantee and also had the necessary power: the unions, and the Kosher Nostra, the Jewish crime syndicate headed by Bugsy Siegel and Meyer Lansky. Via Party comrades, Ethel could make contact with Harry Bridges, the head of the Longshoremen's Union – he was a well-known anti-fascist, and he would like nothing better than an opportunity to beat up Nazis. But if tougher measures were required, it was advisable to turn to the Mobsters. Ben had it on good authority that Siegel and Lansky were already thinking about putting together an armed gang to fight American Nazis, and Bugsy Siegel made no secret of how he viewed Charlie Chaplin: he thought Chaplin was the greatest. For Mr Benjamin Hymen Siegelbaum, Mr Charles Spencer Chaplin was right up there with his mom and the great Yahweh.

Ben's exaggeration made him feel better. He knew his two friends had no connections with the Union or with organised crime, nor did they know anyone who did, not even someone who knew someone who knew someone, but the fact that there might be men out there who were prepared to form a small, quick-witted army around him – that made him feel better. And it made him feel better to give his imagination free rein, and to contemplate the bloody images his mind was projecting on his inner screen with fury and pleasure and without any guilt – after all, they were images of righteous revenge, and he wouldn't be the one in the director's chair.

"And as regards your suicide," said Ben, "There's a sure-fire way of avoiding that: just don't do it!"

That had happened in September. In December, Douglas Fairbanks died in his sleep, of a heart attack. In March of the following year, Ben Eichengreen was beaten up by three men on the beach. His wife Ethel and his friend Herbert were witnesses; they identified his attackers, but none of them were arrested. A few days later, Ben shot himself in the head.

Chaplin couldn't – wouldn't – go to his friend Doug's funeral at the Forest Lawn Memorial Park Cemetery in Glendale, or to his friend Ben's cremation in Carmel. He didn't have the heart to, as he confessed to Joseph Melzer. Nor did he have the heart to write to Ethel Eichengreen. He didn't hear from her again. And he never went back to Carmel.

38

School for Clowns, Clown Town. I grew up in a town in Germany that wasn't bombed during the Second World War. This was due – so our town chronicle says – to the number of inhabitants, which was only just over the number laid down by British Bomber Command, and so Marshall Harris showed mercy, eternal thanks be unto him. Our town is of no real historical interest, and anyone who has been to Dinkelsbühl, Rothenberg ob der Tauber, Bamberg or Wittenberg with their medieval old towns will be disappointed if they expect something similar here. But ours was the only town in Germany – no, for a long time the only town in the world – where there was a school for clowns. The school was founded in 1849, as an expression of repressed anger after the revolution had been crushed. At that time it was called the German Academy for Illusionists and Comedians. From the outset, it was a private enterprise financed by fees and donations. At some point it was granted permission to award diplomas. In the 1910s there was some thought given to dissolving the school and incorporating it into the Royal Academy of Arts in Berlin. But things never got that far; the school was sold, restructured from the ground up, and renamed the School for Clowns. The new owner, Frederic Mehring, was an American whose grandfather came from Germany. He and his family moved back to their old homeland and invested the money here that he'd earned in the steel industry over there. In the twenty years before the Nazis seized power, our town blossomed. There were four theatres – the largest of which held over a thousand people – and half a dozen small stages in basements and outhouses, and everywhere people were performing and teaching comedy, performing and teaching vaudeville. Hypnotists, snake-charmers, jugglers,

speed-talkers, speed-mathematicians, conjurers and joke tellers all
trod the boards here. Every night you could hear laughter in the
streets and alleyways. Frederic Mehring had formed a network
of close relationships over the years: he was friends with Grock,
Dominic Althoff and Carl Godlewski; the escape artist Harry
Houdini was godfather to his son, and he conducted the most ani-
mated debates with Erik Jan Hanussen whenever they met. He was
a charming, eloquent man, who could sell the pleasures of stamp-
collecting to a fire hydrant. Artists came here from all over the
world. The evening in the Stadttheater with the fart-artist Joseph
Pujol was unforgettable – Christian Kraft, Prince Hohenlohe-
Öhringen, and the socialist Georg Ledebour sat peacefully side by
side in the front row, and when the "King of Wind" parped *Yankee
Doodle* in homage to his host, they both had tears in their eyes.

Frederic Mehring's idea was that each artist who performed in
our town should give at least one lesson while they were there,
teaching the next generation "so that laughter and wonder doesn't
die out in our age". Most did it for free, and liked to do it: this place
was unique – it was "Clown Town".

That was the name Charlie Chaplin had given it.

The greatest of all comedians alighted here during his tour of
Europe in 1931, *en route* from Berlin. Every clown in the world
knew of our town, he said, and if he didn't visit us and give at least
one performance and show us at least one of his tricks, it would be
a disgrace and he would never again be able to show his face among
his fellow comedians in America.

On the stage of the Stadttheater, he improvised scenes from his
films: the bread roll dance from *The Gold Rush* and the sequence in
the lion cage from *The Circus* – without the lion, of course – and the
final scene from *City Lights*, in which the flower girl realises who
her benefactor is – without the flower girl, of course. In between
he told stories from his life. Most people in the audience couldn't
speak any English, "but Mr Chaplin speaks a language that requires

no words, and the words that he does speak are music", as it said in our local paper. Somebody brought a cello on stage and Chaplin played melodies from his films, which he had composed himself. The evening lasted over two hours, and afterwards the audience got to their feet and applauded, "and refused to stop for a long time".

The following day, Chaplin held a seminar for children at the School for Clowns. One of the little boys was my father. The trick he learnt that morning was something he performed all his life, for anyone who came to visit us. The "trick" was nothing more than a particular posture, which until then you could only observe in Charlie, the Tramp. Normally a stick, even if it's only a thin cane, serves to take a person's weight off the leg he's standing on. When he puts his weight on his right leg, he holds the stick in his right hand. But Chaplin holds it in his left. When we look at him, we sense that something is not as it should be, but we don't know what. His posture confuses us: this man is defying the laws of gravity. He shows us things outside their context. We are perplexed: is the world not as stable as physics and the people in charge would like us to think it is?

Not a word was spoken during the lesson. The participants had to take off their shoes. Everyone had brought a stick. The pupils were also to refrain from laughing. The clown does not laugh. His own laughter is subtracted from the audience's. As a memento of the morning Chaplin gave everyone a photo of the Tramp, *not* leaning on his cane. He wrote his name across the picture.

There was also an adult at the seminar. Just one. A short, fat, rather older man with a loud snuffle, wearing a black suit with a heavy watch chain attached to his waistcoat. He proved to be the least skilled of them all. Chaplin pointed out his clumsiness by mim-icking it: in truth, it was skill. This man couldn't manage to shake things free of their context. He knew too much about them. He was too skilled. But in the clown's world, he was too unskilled. The method of the clown consists of healing madness with madness. Be unskilled! This is what he tells us. And what he means is: don't let them get you down! If you walk down the up escalator, do it with a sense of grandeur! If you hold your walking stick in the wrong hand, do it with absolute certainty!

Chaplin asked my father – the most skilled of the unskilled – to give the gentleman some extra tuition. The gentleman had to "stay behind" after class while the snow fell outside and the children were heading off with their toboggans. They practised in the school's mirrored hall. The man spoke no German, so my father used his hands and feet and facial expressions to explain how to be unskilled in a skilled way. My father was just nine years old. He did a very good job.

There was a rumour in the town – which all his life my father claimed was true – that this stranger was none other than Winston Churchill. And Churchill *was* in Germany at the time, there is proof of that. I don't know the reason for his trip; he was probably – as on his second trip a few months later with his family – doing research for his Marlborough book. Or perhaps he'd just come to see his friend Charlie – even, perhaps, to study the *method of the clown* with him.

By way of thanks for his tutelage, the gentleman wrote my father a note on the reverse of Chaplin's photograph:

Thank you, my friend Robert,
I will not forget you and your pretty little town
God bless the clowns!
Your faithful student.

Admittedly, he didn't sign his name.

My father had the note analysed by three different graphologists. The first didn't believe it was Churchill's handwriting; the second was convinced these four lines were written by none other than the former British prime minister; the third thought this was somewhere between possible and probable.

My father never said it. He was a naive man through and through. One of those rare people who know they are naive; one of the even rarer people who cannot be hurt by that knowledge. He would have liked to have been a clown. Had the talent for it, too. He was glad to see his son become one. He never said it, no, but I know, I *know* he was convinced he'd saved our home town from destruction. – *God bless the clowns!*

PART FIVE

39

William Knott kept the fact that he was married a secret from his master, and he kept the nature of his service a secret from his wife. He lied to his master that he had separated from his fiancée shortly before the wedding, having admitted to himself that he didn't love her, and he fibbed to his wife that it was his duty to note down what the prime minister said off the record, and to order these notes by date and topic, because Churchill intended to use them for his memoirs one day. He told her the reason he almost never had any time for her now was that his master was almost always saying things off the record.

To my father, he was honest. Knott's first letter repeated the grandiloquent confession he'd made to him – a complete stranger – during their conversation in Aachen: "For thirty-five years, I have been lying: that is my story, and it is my contribution to the history of the twentieth century." He initiated the correspondence in order to finally set things straight. It was William Knott who made the suggestion; my father would have been too shy. He was content with having lunched with the *"very private* private secretary to a *very prime* prime minister"*, and then taken a stroll with him in the Westpark and asked him a few questions, on exclusively political and historical themes – my father had no interest in psychological matters.

"For thirty-five years, I have been lying," William Knott burst out during this walk. (Later, he recalled that the mechanical, colourless way my father spoke – written English translated into sound – made it easier to confide in him, as if he were confiding in the anonymous air. I should like to add: my father also had an expressionless face, with a suspicious similarity to Buster Keaton's physiognomy; suspicious because very few people who knew Keaton believed that that was just the way nature had made him. They always felt for some inexplicable reason that they were having their leg pulled.)

In his very first letter, Knott granted my father a glimpse into "the innermost chamber of my heart" – "The lie has become a second, or rather a first, existence for me. I live like an immigrant who has learned to speak another language and has forgotten his own. I think in this foreign language, I even dream in it. I lie when I don't need to. When I'm travelling, I telephone my wife, and without being asked I mention that I am wearing the blue suit, when I can see the trouser legs and sleeves of the beige one in front of me. I say I've been to dinner when I've been out for a walk. I say I went to the cinema when I spent the whole evening sitting on a bench by the lake, feeding the swans. Even when I am telling the truth, I speak with the accent of the lie."

My father wanted to be close to someone who for a time had been close to the man he revered. William Knott wanted to be close to someone who could help him get away from this same man. The things William Knott told my father in all those long letters about his time with Winston Churchill – most of which my father had no desire to know – were supposed to unspool the thread that would lead him back into his own life.

William Knott was born on 22 May 1911, in Lambeth, behind the knee of the Thames. His father held a senior position in City Hall, and his mother taught in a primary school and gave piano lessons. William studied physics, though he gave up his degree when he was offered a position as an engineer in the newly-created television department of the BBC. After England declared war on Germany – two days after the German Wehrmacht's assault on Poland – Churchill gave an address on television. The prime minister, Neville Chamberlain, had brought him into the cabinet: the long spell in the wilderness was over, and Winston returned to the office of First Lord of the Admiralty. John Reith, the director of the BBC, decided that people out there should hear Winston and see Winston – Winston Churchill, not Neville Chamberlain. The new old head of the navy had never spoken on television before. The camera made him nervous, as did the make-up he had to wear, the lights, the people, the fuss, everyone treating him like the Messiah – nobody was interested in what any other politician had to say about England becoming embroiled in another war, they wanted Winston, Winston, Winston, only he understood what it meant to wage a war – all of this made him nervous. That day of all days he had dropped his denture on the tiles of the bathroom floor, bending it so much that it now fitted badly and made him hiss more than usual when he spoke. This made him particularly nervous. Somebody should call a dentist, he said, get him to come immediately and bend the thing back into shape, the morale of the British people was at stake here. He saw a young man in the crew shake his head. He pointed at him and asked him rather abruptly why he was shaking his head. The young man came over, bent down and whispered in his ear that he mustn't change a thing – under no circumstances should he change anything. That was exactly how the future prime minister of a country at war should speak to the people: hissing like a dangerous snake. The future prime minister? That's right, the future prime minister. So he spoke with a hiss. There wasn't a single member of the crew who didn't feel a shudder run down their spine. That young man, the BBC engineer – he was somebody the commander wanted at his side. He lured him away from the BBC. Which is to say: he requisitioned him. The next day William Knott embarked upon his highly remarkable service with Winston Churchill. A few months later, on 10 May 1940, Churchill was elected prime minister. He formed a National Government and took charge of the Ministry of Defence, which was now a war ministry. That same day, Germany began its Western offensives, with attacks on Luxembourg, Belgium and Holland.

William Knott, who had just turned twenty-nine, was Churchill's private private secretary. He was introduced as such, and that
was how he introduced himself as well. His salary – he was now
earning less than he had done at the BBC – was paid from his
employer's own pocket.

The private private secretary had no correspondence to answer and
no appointment diary to keep. He didn't have to take phone calls,
and his presence was not always required at the prime minister's
meetings. If anyone asked him exactly what he did, he was to say:
"Everything". He should then take a much more aggressive tone
and ask: "And you? Who are you to ask such a question? What's
your interest in the matter? Who put you up to this? I shall have
to report you." And he should take this approach with everyone,
no exceptions: self-confident, arrogant, looking down his nose at
them. Not with Clementine, obviously. But he could do it with
Randolph. Diana and Mary were smart enough not to ask any
questions.

Churchill hid nothing from him. "You are to look after me," he
said, as he showed him the little room that had been cleared out
for him at 10 Downing Street (he also had a room at Chequers,
the prime minister's traditional country seat, and at Chartwell).
"Neither I nor England can afford to have me fall prey to the black
dog." And he gave him the lowdown on this animal. "If, in spite of
your efforts, I should still find an opportunity to shoot myself, you
will take the gun, wipe off my finger prints and claim you are a mur-
derer hired by Hitler. At least I will still be of some use as a martyr.
That sort of thing carries some weight in war. Nothing motivates
and mobilises people like a martyr. Not forever, admittedly. Not
even for very long. But hopefully long enough to find a successor.
They will probably execute you. That comes with the job. So look
after me well. You're looking after yourself at the same time. A lot
depends on you. If people learn that Winston Churchill has taken

his own life, then nothing will stand in Hitler's way. It will be the end of England. It will be the end of civilisation."

That was exactly what Churchill had said, wrote Knott in his first letter to my father. In the beginning, the prime minister found an hour every day to talk to him.

"The two of us," the boss said, "are joined by a single bond: the truth. You are the only person to whom I will tell the truth and nothing but the truth. And you must do the same with me. Can I rely on that?"

"You can rely on that," replied his very private private secretary.

"And everything we say to each other between these four walls: lie about it, to everyone. Can I rely on that?"

"You can rely on that."

40

Alcohol was the director of Churchill's life. "A director, though, not a dictator," he punned. "The people who mix those two up are our enemies." William Knott suggested structuring his drinking. He didn't mean that the prime minister should drink less; it was just a matter of keeping an overview of when he would drink and when he wouldn't, during this exceptional period. Every morning after breakfast – which master and servant *always* took separately – Knott would hand him half a sheet of writing paper on which he had entered the drinking times for that day. Churchill never demanded more time – or less, of course.

There was an ugly argument over the issue of alcohol with Churchill's new physician, Lord Moran. "He was shorter than me by a head, and still he managed to look down on me." His task was similar to William Knott's: to be there for the prime minister, exclusively and at all times. Some cabinet members were so convinced Winston was indispensable that they believed his health had to be monitored constantly, as Lord Moran writes in his memoirs. He knew precisely what they were "concerned" about; he himself found the quantities of alcohol consumed by the prime minister (the PM, as he calls him throughout the book) more than a trifle concerning. During a thorough physical examination – in the presence of William Knott, he had insisted on that – Churchill responded to the question of exactly how much he drank with: "A bottle of champagne in the morning, and one in the evening. Whisky, watered down during the day and straight in the evening – one or two bottles. And of course wine with dinner, and brandy after." And, naked as he was, he turned to his secretary. "Is that right, Willnot, or am I a bottle short?" While the PM got dressed behind the folding screen, the doctor took the secretary to one side, rather too roughly, and asked him – or as Knott put it, ordered him – to visit him at his practice. He noted down the address and an appointment on a prescription sheet and tucked it into Knott's coat pocket.

"Lord Moran was impertinent because he was envious," writes Knott. "He didn't even offer me a seat when I arrived at his practice. He accused me of currying favour with the PM." It was well known, he said, that during his long period of absence from politics, Churchill had developed a soft spot for hard-drinking members of the lower classes. Because they couldn't tell the difference between happiness and unhappiness, and could therefore be tormented by neither the one nor the other. All of London, said Lord Moran, knew that "on certain nights" the great descendant of Marlborough went about with draymen and other riffraff. There had to be an end to it. England was at war! Knott replied: firstly, most draymen were not riffraff; his parents' next-door neighbour Benjamin Winkler was a drayman and a respectable fellow through and through, a family man and a philosopher who could most certainly tell the difference between happiness and unhappiness; and secondly, as for himself, he never touched a drop. He had drunk less in his whole life than "my boss" did in a single day; and in any case, "my boss" was old enough to decide what and how much he drank, and as long as he didn't drink all day without a break, it hurt neither him nor England. After all, "my boss" had reached the age of sixty-six and was still in the best of health.

"Oh yes?" said Lord Moran. "And how do you know that? Are you a doctor? A colleague of mine, are you? Where did you study? What's your specialism?"

William Knott looked him straight in the eye from under half-closed lids and said: "And you? Who are you to ask me such questions? What's your interest in the matter? Who put you up to this? I shall have to report you."

At which Lord Moran turned a deathly white.

A little while later – Churchill was at a meeting of the Chiefs of Staff Committee and William Knott was waiting outside the door in an armchair (which a House of Commons attendant had carried down the long corridor on the PM's orders) – Knott suddenly found himself surrounded by five men in top hats and tails, who smiled at him, and even lowered their heads, though it was admittedly only the suggestion of a bow. They stood in front of him like a black wall, fanning out their coats so he couldn't be seen by passers-by. First, they apologised for the doctor's behaviour. Lord Moran really hadn't known what good work he was doing, they said. He nodded. Went to get up. They took a step closer and leant over him. He had no need to be afraid of them, they said. He wasn't afraid of anybody, he said. Well, that wasn't very clever of him, they said: the whole world was afraid of Adolf Hitler, for instance; only stupid people weren't afraid of anyone. Very well then, he was afraid of Hitler too. A man who was working for the good of the country should be afraid, they said. That was just some friendly advice, they said. Did he remember a particular turn of phrase that Lord Moran had used in connection with the PM and his lifestyle – "certain nights"? Mhm, he did remember that. Did he know what Lord Moran meant by it? No, he didn't. Could he guess what Lord Moran meant by it? He didn't answer that.

"Our concern, then, or call it our fear," said one of the men, whom he judged to be the eldest – and now he no longer sounded friendly – "is that you, Mr Knott, are supporting the PM in his dark drive, or whatever one calls this unpleasant folly dreamed up by some Austrian clever-clogs with too much time on his hands – that you are even urging him on in this direction. What do you think England is? A debating society? A whimsical tea party? A backwater full of old codgers? A racecourse? Why do you think William the Conqueror was called William the Bastard? We know why. Because he *was* a bastard. When someone comes to us with morality and religion, we found a new church and smash the old one into smithereens. Why do you think more blood flows in Shakespeare's plays than runs in the veins of the whole audience? Because the English delight in chopping off heads, cutting throats, putting out eyes, stabbing the women and children of our enemies, poisoning brothers and nephews and locking up other relatives and letting them rot. If someone stands in our way, we don't just kill him – no, we destroy everything around him, as far as his eye has seen. We're not playing Dr Jekyll against Mr Hyde here, Mr Knott, we're playing United Kingdom against German Reich. Winston Churchill is our most senior soldier. We won't tolerate somebody putting a bee in his bonnet. Hitler is right: our PM has no soul. There's nothing there to be stimulated on *certain nights*. Quit your service! You have no master in this house. No one needs you here. We could drive over you without even noticing!"

He got up without a word, William Knott writes, pushed past the men and went to stand on the other side of the door. Remarkably, that seemed to confuse them. They looked at each other, tutted and hurried off. Parliamentary ravens.

That evening he reported the incident to his boss. Churchill clapped him on the shoulder and laughed. "Excellent strategy!" he cried. "Don't debate. Change where you're standing, but not your standpoint!"

In truth, the ravens had intimidated him. He could think of nothing to throw back at them. In his agitation he had even forgotten the words Churchill had drummed into him. And the reason he had gone to stand on the other side of the door rather than taking to his heels was simply that his knees had turned to butter.

Churchill knew that there were a few people – particularly in the ranks of his own party – who thought him "inconsistent", and a few who thought him "unpredictable", and a few who just thought he was mad. Interestingly, they were the same people who believed they had a great enough hold on the state to push him forward as a figurehead, beloved of the people, while they pulled the strings behind the scenes – for the good of England, naturally. To remove any doubt about who had the final word from now on, he issued the following decree:

> There must be total clarity in this matter: all instructions issued by me will be in written form, or will be immediately confirmed in writing, and I shall take no responsibility for matters relating to national defence upon which I have made decisions, if these decisions are not set down in writing.

He added a hand-written note:

> *This also applies above all to staffing decisions relating to my person. That is to say: those employed for my protection, drivers, cooks and secretaries.*

The prime minister greatly reduced his alcohol consumption. He discussed this with William Knott, displaying the same serious-ness with which he had listened and responded to his Chiefs of Staff an hour before, as they gave him their report on the situation in France. The drinking diary sheets from this period show that his breakfast champagne was limited to a single glass. He gave up brandy after dinner entirely, and doubled the amount of water in his whisky during the day, effectively halving the quantity he con-sumed. In his letters to my father, William Knott emphasised that this had nothing to do with repentance or resolution; it was because of an increase in work – and even in a desk job, more work entails a greater number of hand movements, leaving the prime minister fewer opportunities to reach for a glass to drink from, and a bottle to top up his glass; his mouth, too, was significantly more occupied with speaking than it used to be. ("Which," adds William Knott, "those close to the prime minister assured me was hardly possi-ble, but which was in fact the case, as they were forced to admit after spending a morning in his presence.") Even though his days were longer, his alcohol consumption was lower. The prime minister slept less than before he was elected. But he slept more deeply. And he didn't dream. He "had no need for cheering dreams," he said (and wrote in *The Second World War*), "facts are better than dreams".

41

The air raids on England began in September. Following a British counter-strike on Berlin, Göring raised the pressure, and from then on, two hundred German bombers thundered over London every night. The city was unprepared. Churchill had taken every opportunity in the preceding years to call for rearmament from the back benches, and had had to put up with being called a warmonger, even by his own people. Now these people were expecting to feel his wrath. "They are expecting to feel my wrath," he told William Knott. "And they have enough imagination and experience to work out for themselves all the things I might do to them. So I say nothing. Anything more would be a waste." But of course he didn't say nothing. He railed against the pitiful efforts of the British night fighters and flak guns. He berated General Pile, the head of Anti-Aircraft Command, as the general sat in front of him, twisting his cap in his hands until the tears began to run down his cheeks. After that, the number of anti-aircraft guns in the capital was doubled within forty-eight hours. The cannonade may have brought down no more than a few enemy planes, but it gave London great satisfaction and fuelled its zeal. German spies reported to Berlin that after some initial confusion, life in the city of eight million had more or less returned to normal – to which Göring and his officers reacted with rage, astonishment and admiration. Hitler threatened: "If they attack our cities, we will raze theirs to the ground!"

The government buildings around Whitehall were also hit. The ministerial offices and the prime minister's private rooms were moved to the more solid government buildings on Storey's Gate. A little room was made available there for William Knott (an application was both made and approved by Churchill). A day bed and a

study were also reserved for Frederick Lindemann; he was Churchill's closest advisor on the development and expansion of the air
force, and the prime minister insisted on having him within shouting distance, in case an idea came to him in the middle of the night
and he wanted to discuss it.

Cabinet meetings were held every evening in the basement of the
prime minister's private apartment, often by candlelight, whenever
the power failed and the diesel generator had to be repaired once
again. Churchill commanded an army of informants, meaning he
knew just as much about the work of individual departments as the
minsters responsible for them. This led to tensions when one minister or another felt he had been passed over, and it culminated in a
heated debate with threats of resignation when the prime minister
merged the Home Office and the Ministry for State Security with
no prior discussion, and reallocated the jobs there. The day would
come, people joked – and they weren't always joking – when there
would be only one ministry, *his* ministry, and that would be the day
the roles of prime minister and king would be merged.

Every Tuesday, Churchill went to luncheon at Buckingham
Palace with George VI, to discuss the latest developments and take
care of state business. Several times they had to pick up their plates
and glasses and go down to the air raid room, which was still being
finished. Churchill came in uniform, which bothered the king at
first. Could he carry a submachine gun, Churchill asked. Of course
not, the king retorted indignantly. The monarch regarded the submachine gun as a vulgar weapon, a weapon of mass destruction,
unseemly and impractical in chivalrous fighting. Churchill talked
him into taking a lesson at the shooting range. Afterwards, the king
raved about "his" Thompson, his voice falsetto with excitement.
The next time he visited, Churchill brought a carbine, a pistol and
an American hunting knife with him. And a year later, when the
significantly lighter Sten Gun was developed, a British submachine
gun with a muzzle velocity three times higher than the American

version, the first one off the production line went to the king, and the second to his prime minister.

William Knott writes that he had the impression Churchill had stopped sleeping. He himself never slept for more than four hours on Blitz nights, but when he got up at five in the morning and tiptoed across the corridor to the improvised bathroom, he would hear the prime minister droning a song through his cigar. The door to his study was open, so he could give his orders to whomever he wanted at any time. On one of the nights when the bombing was heaviest, the boss woke Knott and Professor Lindemann, and the three of them went up to the roof and watched the spectacle from beside the dome. It looked like the end of the world. As though the city was screaming, he said, that's what it was like. There was no emotion on Professor Lindemann's face, but Churchill cheered. Wearing his uniform jacket over his pyjamas, his officer's cap on his head, he stood at the parapet, and at every hit he cried out: "Tenfold in return! Tenfold in return!" The majority of Pall Mall was on fire. Fires were blazing in St James's Street and Picadilly. On the other side of the Thames they could see a chain of conflagrations. Churchill, his wife, Professor Lindemann and William Knott spent the nights that followed in the basement. Against Churchill's will. "England is our ship, and I am its captain," he said. Lindemann said that was sentimental nonsense, England didn't need dead heroes; it needed living strategists to wreak revenge.

The Germans lacked the resources to bomb a city like London to smithereens. But they had enough resources to wound and destroy souls. In addition to the conventional explosive bombs, the planes dropped delayed-action bombs. They burrowed into the earth, vanished into houses and back gardens, and had to be found, dug out and defused – if they could be defused before they exploded. It was painstaking, enervating, dangerous, demoralising. The uncertainty wore people down, drove them mad. Amid the general noise of an air raid, nobody dared say if and where a "silent" bomb had fallen. They could be anywhere. There was a rumour they were armed with nails. There was a rumour they were brightly painted to attract children. When lives were lost, people blamed the state's civil defence. That bred discord. It was intended to breed discord. This was psychological warfare. Churchill quickly drafted a detailed organisational plan to deal with this new threat: in every city, town and district, he ordered special companies of volunteers to be set up, who would search for ticking bombs, dig them out and defuse them. Young men and young women were given a crash course – in a discipline that even the instructors didn't understand. "Volunteers," Churchill writes laconically in his memoirs, "pressed forward for the deadly game". England had its first martyrs. People said: "If only we'd listened to Winston earlier!"

Churchill appointed Herbert Morrison, an experienced Labour politician who had once been a fierce opponent of his, as Minister of Supply and chief fire officer for London, demanding nothing less of him than a reduction of deaths and injuries by at least half. Not twenty hours later, he summoned him to the "war office" (his bedroom) in the middle of the night to hear his response. They were working on it. That wasn't good enough. So the prime minister laid out his own plan: an air raid shelter, simple and quick to manufacture, easy to transport, and cheap. He had even prepared a drawing, to scale, in minute detail. When? It was a thing to be mass-produced, a large steel box with strong side walls made of wire mesh, shaped rather like a kitchen table, and "capable of bearing the weight of the rubble from a small house." The objects should be placed in cellars, in an easily accessible spot. There would be room for five to six adults or eight to nine children in each.

"But those are cages," said Morrison. "You want to put our people in cages?"

"Like wild animals, yes," said the prime minister. "The Germans have made wild animals of us. Shut a wild animal in a cage, and it gets even wilder. What do you have against Britons becoming beasts in such times as these? The state will of course cover the cost of production. Prepare a motion for it! Right now! You can sit over there at the typewriter. I'll approve the motion and sign it. The people can keep the cages. After the war they can do what they like with them. I'm already curious to see what they come up with."

To put a halt to his chief fire officer's head-shaking, Churchill suggested calling the cages Morrison Shelters. "The king will give you an honour for that." Which he duly did.

On 14 November 1940, Göring gave the order for Operation Moonlight Sonata. That night, 568 people died in the city of Coventry, and more than four thousand houses were destroyed. Goebbels spoke of "coventrification", meaning the destruction of cities from the air. Marshall Arthur Harris, head of RAF Bomber Command from 1942, would later speak of "hamburgisation" following the obliteration of Hamburg in a fire storm. Cologne, Kassel, Dortmund, Darmstadt, Frankfurt, Pforzheim, Dresden – it's a long list – were hamburgised. By the end of the war, the majority of German cities were eighty or ninety per cent destroyed, and some had been flattened completely – Lindemann's method.

42

At that time, William Knott writes, Churchill was living like three people, who divided up the day between them. And he tried to fill every last bit of breathing room in the corset of his day with meaningful activity – and by meaningful, as he frequently lectured his very private secretary, he didn't mean politics, and certainly not the war, but "occupying oneself with beauty". When he had dinner with the Canadian foreign minister at the Turkish Pera Palas Hotel, newly built before the war (in December it was hit by an SC 2000 bomb, collapsed, and was never rebuilt), he was quite taken with the little fountains in the toilets, which were installed above the sinks in place of taps and were operated by pressing a button. The point of dispensing water in this manner, he concluded, could only be that when one drank from the tap, one wouldn't come into contact with the germs of the previous user. The meeting with the Canadian was his eighth appointment that day, and he had another three ahead of him, one of which was with the general manager of the Rolls Royce factories. Still, he couldn't resist: he hurried back to the dining room, fetched a notebook and pencil from his pocket, asked his guest to excuse him for another five minutes, went back to the toilets and drew the tap – that would be the very thing for the bathroom of the guesthouse at Chartwell, when the house was extended after the war. As he organised the defence of English cities, planned the destruction of Germany, pressed the American president with gentle but constant exhortations to enter the war, as he took care of the usual state business, which was the same in wartime as it was in peacetime, as he travelled to the launches of new warships and new aeroplanes; in short, as he did the work of captaining the ship of England, he was also planning and drawing and building cardboard models of this guesthouse. On top of this, he developed a system for reorganising his library: hole-punched index cards, hanging on several thin metal rods, which could be pushed back or pulled out to find key words – the primitive ancestor of the search engine.

Once, after a long cabinet meeting, he called William Knott into his office. He told the secretary he didn't want to be disturbed for the next hour. Even if Herr Hitler himself came knocking to offer Germany's surrender, he would have to wait. He shut the door and told William Knott to take a seat opposite him. That was their very private seating arrangement: knee to knee. Churchill's alternative to Freud's couch.

The boss seemed unusually serious, writes William Knott.

Churchill began: "When one man dies, the whole world dies. Do you know that saying?"

He didn't know that saying.

"It's what the Jews say. What do you think of it, Willnot?"

He replied that he couldn't fault it.

"It's a good saying," Churchill went on. "We must never stop thinking that way, Willnot. Especially in wartime." He pulled out his notepad from the inside pocket of his coat. "We must never stop thinking that way," he repeated. "That was something which became clear to me during this incredibly dull meeting just now. We talk and talk and talk. Even in the midst of war, Halifax can't keep that note of sarcasm out of his voice – every word he utters sounds like it should have "so-called" in front of it – the so-called agreement, the so-called treaty, the so-called war. Clement, precise and succinct as ever. And then Kingsley Wood starts up, in his slow, deliberate manner, and after four words I know what the seventeenth word is going to be, and it makes me think, I hope the bomb that's going to fall on our heads would hurry up and fall before Mr Wood has finished saying his piece – everyone will have forgotten what he was talking about by the time he gets to the point, to the so-called point, as Halifax would say. But if that bomb does hit us, I thought, then all these worlds will be obliterated. Do you see, Willnot, everyone has said something, something unimportant or important. We tend to think that in the face of death, everything is unimportant. But that's not true. These last words, however banal and boring they may be, suddenly contain everything. Everything. Life. Life, plain and simple. They were talking, and now they're lying dead. They formed words, and these were their last words, and they didn't know it. Imagine, Willnot, if a poet knew how to use words as if they were being spoken for the last time. Wouldn't that be the very definition of poetry? To speak as if it were the last time! Each word a treasure from a lost world. Proof that there was life here, once. That's exactly what poetry is. If anyone tries to give you another definition, box his ears! I couldn't help it, I wrote down what these gentlemen were saying. And I set it out as a poem in free verse."

In October Sarah returned from the States, alone. Her husband, Vic Oliver, had too good a job in Hollywood to accompany her, so a "certain newspaper" reported. It was midday, the sun shone above the city, and people were waiting for the evening air raids, using the peace and quiet and the last warm rays to go outside and shop, or to take a stroll, or just to sit in the sun. Churchill beckoned William Knott over – he had seen him in the hallway of 10 Downing Street – and asked him to go up to the roof with him: he needed to talk. The boss's face was moist and bluish white. Up on the roof he showed him the article. The impertinent hacks at this particular paper had not only placed "too good a job" in inverted commas, but also "her husband". The editor, Harold Moore, was a personal enemy of Churchill's, a Nazi sympathiser who had congratulated Hitler the year before on his invasion of Czechoslovakia. The final sentence of the article said that Victor Israel (sic!)

Oliver most likely wanted to get shot of "our" prime minister's daughter, who was known to be as stubborn as a mule; and to quote the article: "The way he is going about it is shabby, of course, as is only to be expected from his kind; on the other hand, it is perfectly understandable."

"It's impossible for her to divorce him now," said Churchill. "She wanted to divorce him, and now she can't."

The boss told him, William Knott writes, that for the past year he had been paying a detective to follow Sarah's husband in Hollywood, hoping to uncover something that could be used against him in a divorce. And he did uncover something. He uncovered more than enough. But that was all worthless now.

William Knott said nothing.

"You think it was dishonourable of me to spy on my son-in-law?"

Again, William Knott said nothing.

"I knew she would be unhappy with him. I knew it. Just as I knew there would be war between Britain and Germany. There was war. She was unhappy. If you had a daughter, Willnot, wouldn't you do something dishonourable to free her from her unhappiness?"

And this time he replied: "Yes, I would."

"A rotten, dirty, dishonourable thing?"

"The rottenest, dirtiest, most dishonourable thing."

The prime minister reached up to his head and pulled it down to his and pressed it to him. For a long time.

They sat down on the wooden bench that Ed Thomas, the valet, had dragged up to the roof weeks earlier so that the prime minister and his guests could sit in comfort and watch the air raids. The street below teemed with people, some on bicycles, some pulling handcarts, women with prams, the milkman with his horse and cart. Couples arm-in-arm. Hurrying loners. Strolling idlers. Music was coming from somewhere, a brass band. A policeman's whistle silenced the birds, but only for a little while; a chorus of sparrows soon began twittering again.

"I haven't told you my whole life story yet, Willnot," said
Churchill. "And we probably won't have time for that, now. But
I've told you more than anyone else. I mean, beyond the things that
are general knowledge round here. And let me add that the roof is
out of bounds to everyone from now on. You and I, Willnot, are
the exceptions. Just you and I. If I can't find you, I have to know
that you'll be up here. Can I ask that of you?"

"Yes."

"Very well then."

"May I ask something of you, Sir?" he said to the prime minister.
"Please would you stop calling me Willnot? My name is William
Knott."

43

On one of those nights when the sirens were droning and the bombs were detonating – William Knott writes – he couldn't sleep. He went up to the roof and found the boss there, sitting in front of his easel in the dark, painting. Without whisky! It was so dark that he couldn't possibly have been able to tell the colours apart. Now and then a flash would light up the sky, but all it did was blind them. Churchill told him to sit down and watch him. He dipped a brush in the paint without looking, and applied it to the canvas in fast, sweeping strokes. Did he know Kandinsky's "Untitled Watercolour"? he asked. It was said to be the first abstract picture in the history of art. But he didn't believe that. He didn't believe Kandinsky meant to paint an abstract picture. Nobody means to do such a thing. Why would they. His theory was that Kandinsky had had no light, just as he had no light now. Of course Kandinsky had wanted to paint something figurative. But he couldn't see anything. And so what came out, came out, namely the "Untitled Watercolour". Theory was applied to things after the fact. Always. The same in art as it was in politics. And it was just the same in war. In battle, inexplicable chance events made the difference between victory and defeat. First people said history was God's plan; then they said history was created by people. And what if neither of these were true? The theologians' answers had always seemed absurd to him, if only because of the words in which they were dressed – spirit instead of bread, providence instead of the invention of winter clothing. Even as a child he had been marked out by a failure to be beguiled by shadow puppetry.

"Wouldn't it be fun to play God – to raze the wonderful city of Cologne to the ground, but leave the cathedral standing? The

Germans would believe it was the hand of their God. But it would be us."

Hitler and his Germans didn't know, or didn't want to know: in the end, their cities would look like abstract paintings. The war was just accelerating the process. Someday everything would look like an abstract painting.

"Mr Knott, it takes a good deal of courage to paint a faithful figurative picture! Abstraction is mere cowardice, it is the artist falling to his knees before transience, it is the recognition of the senselessness in the eternal flow of cause and effect. We must not fall in with the dispirited! Spirit is something only we possess. There is nobody else in the universe who can imagine the unimaginable. But enough said, Mr Knott, enough seen, enough heard! Let's pack up! Let's go!"

Down in the office they looked at the picture together. By then, it was three o'clock in the morning.

"What do you say, William?" the boss asked him. "What shall I call it? Think about it! Please!"

But he didn't know what to say.

That was the end of November.

On the evening of 12 December – it was a date Mr Knott would always remember – there was a scratch at the door. The black dog was there.

William Knott knew what to do.

When he had finally grasped what his task involved – "when a person says to you, look after me, make sure I don't put a bullet in my head, then you hear his words, but you are not immediately clear about the consequences" – he got in touch with a "psychologist". He had to qualify this: not a psychologist in the sense that he had a licence, but not some windbag who would talk a problem into your head and the money out of your pocket. He was a friend of a friend, a man who had patched up many a marriage, alleviated many people's depression, steered many away from the bottle and many back to the Lord. He went to this man – "you Germans might call him a saint" – and told him a sob story about his father contemplating suicide. He asked the man what he should do when the situation became acute. He replied: "Go for a walk. Walk, walk and keep on walking. Walk until he's exhausted."

It was an unusually cold December. That was an advantage. With his own money, William Knott bought a cheap but well-padded long coat, a style that thousands of people wore; a cheap, well-padded hat with long ear flaps; and a scarf and gloves. Not even Mrs Churchill would have recognised the prime minister in this disguise. And luckily she was in Chartwell, tending to Sarah and the greenhouse. William Knott had spent the night at the flat on Storey's Gate, on the mattress outside the open door to Churchill's bedroom.

Churchill was mutely compliant. He sat on his bed and stared at the wall opposite. William Knott switched on the reading lamp. The curtains remained closed. He dressed his boss, saying everything he was doing out loud as he did it – just as the "psychologist" had recommended. It made the patient conscious of reality, and also had a comic effect. He pulled the hat down over Churchill's forehead, wound the scarf around his neck so that only his nose and eyes were visible, helped him into the coat, tugged on the gloves and led him by the arm to the door and out into the street. To the right, there was nobody to be seen; to the left, there was nobody to be seen. The chauffeur was waiting in the car two streets away. He wasn't Churchill's chauffeur, or some other official driver, he was a friend of a friend, whom William Knott had booked in a hurry, spinning him some yarn or other. He pushed his swaddled boss into the back seat, jammed himself in beside him, and they set off. The sun was not yet up.

They drove out of the city and on up the Thames, until they had left the last houses behind them. Then they pulled over and breakfasted at the roadside. William Knott had brought ham and cheese sandwiches, apples and a thermos of tea. The chauffeur turned and watched them – no, he didn't want any, he'd eaten. Churchill had not yet said a single word. William Knott pulled the scarf down under his chin, and handed him a sandwich and a tin cup of steaming tea. He ate and drank in silence. He didn't want to smoke. He shook his head. The secretary hadn't brought any alcohol.

They carried on heading west to the marshy banks of the Thames. William Knott loved this area; his grandfather had lived there, raising horses and repairing saddles. For a second he thought he would like to be a horse. It seemed a good idea to pretend he and his boss were horses, two wild, free horses. He told the chauffeur to wait for them at the same place in four hours' time.

They walked in silence. Churchill kept shaking his head, but he said nothing. The path ran between horse fences. Behind a row of poplars, they could see stables and half-timbered houses. Smoke was rising. A dozen stallions were standing in a trampled clearing, still as statues. Sunbeams, coming through the clouds, fell on their heads. There were a few grey horses, a palomino, some bays with black tails and manes and gracefully curved swan necks.

A motorbike with a sidecar approached them, a man and a woman, both bundled up in thick coats up to their noses, leather caps on their heads, sunglasses masking their eyes. The man eased off the throttle and asked in a wool-muffled voice if he could help them – were they looking for someone? William Knott laughed in a familiar manner, as if he knew the man and the woman, and said he was just taking a pre-Christmas walk with his father, who had grown up here and wanted to ease his homesickness a little – he had arrived from Chicago just a few days ago. As the two of them walked on, Churchill said: "Very good. I could be your father, couldn't I?" He didn't laugh at the tall tale. The "psychologist" had been very insistent that the easiest way to make a depressed person laugh was to tell a third party an audacious lie in his presence. Yes, he had been very insistent. "You have to play the scoundrel a little," he'd said. "Steal a piece of cake when you're with him, lie to a policeman, stick your tongue out at a child behind its mother's back, pretend to be a limping Frenchman or a stutterer. Making the depressed person into your accomplice will gladden his heart. Don't ask me why that should be so. It just is."

William Knott quickened his pace, gradually, so that his boss didn't notice. This was another thing the "psychologist" had advised him to do. He was aiming for total exhaustion; just making him tired wouldn't do. "If a person is forced to think about his bones and muscles, he doesn't think about his soul." In general, the "psychologist" thought the soul didn't exist (which is why William Knott also placed him in inverted commas in his letter).

At one point Churchill asked if he'd told the office where they were – England seemed to be surviving without them. He'd spoken to Paul Ackroyd, one of the secretaries of state from the Defence Ministry, replied William Knott. He'd told him the prime minister was taking a day's holiday in the Bahamas. The prime minister had decided to go on the spur of the moment. There was no need to give a reason – everyone in the office thought the prime minister was in urgent need of at least one day's holiday. The boss didn't laugh at the Bahamas story, either.

When they had been walking for two hours, Churchill said: "This was a good idea of yours. Thank you, William. I'm doing better now. Don't you think?"

On the night of 15 December, William Knott didn't sleep on the floor outside Churchill's door, but on the floor beside Churchill's bed. If the boss wanted to get up, he would have to tread on him. That was the idea. But when he woke up, the boss wasn't in his bed. Nor had he trodden on him. He had tiptoed out of the room. William Knot pulled on his boots and coat, ran up the stairs and climbed the metal ladder to the roof. The boss was standing at the parapet. Barefoot. Bareheaded. In his pyjamas. The air raids had eased off since mid-November. Maybe the Germans were preparing to try a new tactic, having failed to break the courage of the Londoners; or maybe they'd lost interest in Great Britain. When it became known that Hitler had made a pact with Stalin, Churchill had marched along the corridors, gesticulating and grinning. This was the first step towards Germany declaring war on Russia, he prophesied. Either Stalin really was the sly fox he believed him to be, and from now on he would work like the devil to prepare his country for war, or he was just as stupid as the rest of the world, and Russia would soon be overrun by the German Wehrmacht. Churchill took the reduction in German planes over England as a sign that an attack on Russia was imminent – he had announced it to his astonished ministers just a few days previously (before the dog had scratched at the door). The night was not as cold as the nights had been of late, and it was clear and quiet. No fire, no sirens, no cannons, no detonations. A dark city, yes, but a peaceful one.

Without turning to his very private private secretary, he said: "It's not your fault, William. Nobody will say it's your fault. Don't worry, I'm not going to jump. I'm still clear-headed enough to make a decision. I'll step down. Dr Moran will give the press a suitable explanation. I just came up here to see what it would be like."

"What what would be like?" he asked.

"What it would be like if a short, fat man like me were to hit the asphalt on Tothill Street a few days before Christmas. It would be difficult to construct an assassination out of it. Although anything can be constructed. Have I told you that my friend Charlie Chaplin and I are both keen collectors of suicide methods? We think of a method, and at the same time we think of how it would be to use it on ourselves. It can be cheering..."

At that, Knott interrupted his boss and cried out: "Charlie Chaplin is in town! Didn't you know? It was in the paper! He's premiering his new film in three days. It's the funniest film he's ever made. A film about Hitler. People will die laughing!"

The premiere of *The Great Dictator* was to take place in four cinemas at once: the Prince of Wales, the Gaumont Haymarket, the Marble Arch and the London Pavilion. William Knott drove from one cinema to the next. Owen Peters at the Haymarket finally knew – or at least, he was the only one prepared to tell in return for money – where Chaplin was: at the Haydon Studios in Hammer-smith, where he had rented a cutting room for five days. They said he was even sleeping there.

44

When I was still a schoolteacher, because I couldn't live off clowning alone, I wrote sketches for two people, and performed them with a female colleague. I was Pierrot, she was Auguste, with a red nose and oversized checked dungarees. Things were going well. Our weekends were booked up. We were well-matched. I wrote the less funny part of the white-painted know-it-all for myself, and for her I wrote the part of the cunning, intentionally clumsy, sometimes cruel anarchist. She got married, and then things stopped going well. She had a baby, and then things stopped going altogether. For a while I performed solo. But it didn't suit me. In the late eighties, I saw the Australian puppeteer Neville Tranter and his play *Underdog* at a theatre festival in Stuttgart, and I was smitten. I wanted to be like him. I wanted to try partnering a puppet. I had found my calling. And it was so obvious. A man from the other side of the world made me think about my own story.

My mother died when I was five – I only have vague memories of her. My father never got over his loss. He didn't marry again. To console himself and to give me some sense of a family, in the evenings before bed he would act out "The Parents' Conversation about Their Son". That was his impersonal way of putting it. He would hug a pillow, that was my mother, and speak first as himself and then as her. Without changing his voice. There was nothing parodic about it. Sometimes the conversations were funny, sometimes serious; and if they were funny, they weren't meant to be. He would tell my mother what had happened that day, and she would comment on it. He'd ask her advice, and she would give it. Sometimes they disagreed; sometimes they argued, and then he would take offence and stop talking and leave the talking to her until they made up again. He acted it so believably that during the scene it didn't once occur to me that all this wasn't real. When he took offence, he *was* offended, and I would beg him to make up with Mum, or I wouldn't be able to sleep. My father was a great comedian, a great involuntary comedian.

I built and tried out various puppets, all modelled on Neville Tranter's: life-sized with a mouth you could open and close. I made an Auguste, a Harlequin, a Kasper, the egg-headed white clown, and a Buster Keaton. I improvised conversations with them. I couldn't strike the right tone.

Then my father died, and in his papers I found his extensive correspondence with William Knott. I read about Churchill's friendship with Charlie Chaplin. I read that the two of them had formed an alliance against their common enemy, depression. I read how a desperate William Knott had taken Great Britain's supreme commander, incognito, by taxi to the Haydon Studios in Hammersmith, to meet the friend who could help him. I read that they found Chaplin in a heap of cut celluloid, from which the top half of his slender body was protruding – a man who was no less in need of his friend's help than his friend was of his. This was a circumstance neither of them had foreseen: the black dog visiting them both at the same time.

Afraid of the Hearst press, which had more influence on the West Coast than it did on the Eastern seaboard, Chaplin had decided to hold the world premiere of *The Great Dictator* in New York, at the Capitol and Astor theatres. The papers owned by William Randolph Hearst didn't give much thought to the film's aesthetic aspect – they saw it as a disgusting piece of warmongering, commissioned by the Churchill-Roosevelt clique. The East Coast newspapers, by contrast, barely touched on the film's all-too-obvious political dimension, though they were not convinced of its artistic merit. The *New York Times* said that this was perhaps the most significant film ever produced, but the critic was referring to its political impact and the audacity of the enterprise. Otherwise he thought the dialogue feeble – "and no wonder, for Chaplin's first pure talking picture" – the music calamitous, and the "persistent lapses in style" made the film seem muddled. Another reviewer spoke of the picture as a grandiose flop. A third said charitably that it wasn't all that bad, but it could have been better. The final monologue, when the Jewish barber, who has been mistaken for the dictator, makes a radio broadcast calling for peace, tolerance, freedom and hope, was too kitschy for everyone. There was talk of embarrassment, of a monumentally tasteless ending, of the betrayal of an artistic ethos. One critic wrote that the speech had ruined not just the film, but Chaplin's whole career. Klaus Mann blustered that "It has no style, no continuity, no convincing power. [...] It is a ludicrous farce, adorned with turgid editorials. Mr Chaplin's concluding harangue is almost unbearably trite."

Chaplin gave no interviews after the New York premiere. Later, he told Josef Melzer he had felt as though his veins were running with iced water. As though the whole world was laughing him to death. As though he had committed a crime. At first he wanted to cancel the London premiere, but Syd made it clear to him that the financial penalties for that would blow their budget. Then he telegraphed London to rent a studio there, and travelled to England earlier than planned – with the neat, velvet-lined box that Raphael Brooks had given him in his suitcase. In five days, he wanted to completely recut the film. If he worked day and night, he told himself, it could be done. One day before the screening, he realised it couldn't be done. He had cut the copy to pieces. If they had to show the American cut, he didn't want to go out in front of the London audience. He never wanted to go out in front of an audience again.

Before Churchill and William Knott entered the cutting room, Chaplin had just listened to the barber's speech, for the hundredth time.

Hannah, can you hear me? Wherever you are, look up, Hannah. The clouds are lifting. The sun is breaking through. We are coming out of the darkness into the light. We are coming into a new world, a kindlier world, where men will rise above their hate, their greed and brutality. Look up, Hannah. The soul of man has been given wings, and at last he is beginning to fly. He is flying into the rainbow – into the light of hope [...]. Look up, Hannah. Look up.

Churchill came up behind him, laid a hand on his shoulder and said: "It's me, Winston." And he said again: "It's me, Winston."

Chaplin turned round, stood up, and told William Knott he wanted to be alone with his friend. He asked him to wait. To take a seat in his armchair. He took Churchill's hand and led him into the darkroom. The door clicked shut behind them.

And he – he waited, writes William Knott.

I was aware of my father's friendship with William Knott, though not of what the latter's work for Churchill had entailed. Nor had my father ever spoken to me about the extent of their correspondence. And now, as I read the letters – Knott's widow was good enough to send me my father's replies as well – I knew at once that I had to have a very, very long conversation with my father. Yes: now, after his death. Just as he had had a very, very long conversation with my mother after her death. I built a puppet, gave it his features, his hair, his throat, his hands. The only prop on the stage would be a large table, at which my father and I would sit. It would look like I had put my arm around him. In this way I could control the puppet. I wrote the dialogue, asked my former colleague to assist me as co-director and coach. She read the text. Was I sure about this, she asked me. Yes, I said. Why? She said she'd thought the text was going to be a classic clown entrée, only longer. I said: isn't it? My father and I talked about depression; I was the white clown and he was the Auguste. We didn't tell a single joke, we didn't twist a single sentence into a piece of word-play, we didn't say a single risqué word. We left long pauses, heart-rendingly long pauses. But the audience laughed. They laughed so hard that the premiere was twenty minutes longer than the dress rehearsal. The white clown and the Auguste talked about various methods of committing suicide, and various methods of avoiding suicide. And they talked about the *method of the clown*. The white clown told the old Indian creation myth about a god who invents the world out of boredom, by lying on his belly and turning in a circle, scratching a spiral of images and signs into the stone, starting with the division of light and darkness, water and land, and going on to the creation of animals and men out of slime, on to first love, first hatred, the first murder, the first act of forgiveness, the first memory, the first piece of music, the first recognition of a connection. Everything that happens. The story says the world will end when he gets to his belly, and can't go on drawing. The Auguste told the story of the friendship between the great statesman and the great actor; how the two men fought the black dog together, and fought Hitler together, one with laughter, the other with war. The white clown threw in the story about Theodor W. Adorno and his missing essay "Framework for a Theory of the Comic", and said that in his hour of bitterest despond in American exile, the philosopher lay on his belly and wrote a letter to himself. The Auguste spoke of God, in whom he believed, and said that God sometimes allowed himself to be deceived, by white clown puppeteers for example, and that He wasn't angry with them, even if they didn't believe in Him. The white clown called the Auguste a stupid Auguste, and the Auguste fell silent for a long time and stared out into the blackness. "Please, talk to me," the white clown said to the Auguste. "Talk to me, or I won't be able to sleep tonight!" Then the Auguste kissed him and told him the story about how the greatest of all comedians had taught him how to hold his cane in the wrong hand, and how he, the most skilful of the unskilled, tutored a short, fat, rather older man with a loud snuffle, wearing a black suit with a heavy watch chain attached to his waistcoat, teaching him how to be unskilled, as snow fell outside the windows and the boys and girls headed off with their toboggans to the hill outside our town – a town that was big enough for Professor Lindemann's planes, but remained intact throughout the war. There is only one way to measure comedy: laughter. The white clown, whose hand allowed the Auguste to move, heard it in the auditorium. He couldn't see anything: the spotlights were pointing at him.

William Knott waited. He put his ear to the door. After an hour – he thought it had been an hour – he pushed the latch down and opened the door. He saw a table, where the statesman and the clown were sitting, their heads close together. They looked at him and blinked in the light.